THE
PLAYMAKER

THE
PLAYMAKER

Alex O'Brien

James Lorimer & Company Ltd., Publishers
Toronto

James Lorimer & Company Ltd., Publishers acknowledges funding support from the Ontario Arts Council (OAC), an agency of the Government of Ontario. We acknowledge the support of the Canada Council for the Arts, which last year invested $153 million to bring the arts to Canadians throughout the country. This project has been made possible in part by the Government of Canada and with the support of Ontario Creates.

Cover design: Tyler Cleroux
Cover image: Shutterstock

Library and Archives Canada Cataloguing in Publication

O'Brien, Alex, 1963-, author
        The playmaker / Alex O'Brien.

(Sports stories)
Issued in print and electronic formats.
ISBN 978-1-4594-1395-5 (softcover).--ISBN 978-1-4594-1396-2 (EPUB)

        I. Title.

PS8629.B72P53 2019   jC813'.6   C2018-905309-7
                                              C2018-905310-0

Published by: Distributed in Canada by: Distributed in the US by:
James Lorimer &   Formac Lorimer Books   Lerner Publisher Services
Company Ltd., Publishers   5502 Atlantic Street   1251 Washington Ave. N.
117 Peter Street, Suite 304 Halifax, NS, Canada   Minneapolis, MN, USA
Toronto, ON, Canada   B3H 1G4   55401
M5V 0M3   www.lernerbooks.com
www.lorimer.ca

Printed and bound in Canada.
Manufactured by Friesens Corporation in Altona, Manitoba,
Canada in December 2018.
Job # 250166

For Terry King and Chico Ralf, two coaches who believed in a young hockey player and made a difference in her life.

Contents

1 TRYOUTS

Zoey Findley didn't want to leave anything to chance. It was the third and final tryout. She stepped onto the ice and raced ahead — brown ponytail swaying below her helmet. She skated as if she had to win the warm-up. She was nervous and felt out of place. But she wasn't going to let that hold her back. She'd been playing pickup hockey on an outdoor rink in Innisfil for six years. There was no girls' hockey in Innisfil and she was looking to improve her skills and find better competition. So she really wanted to make the Barrie Sharks bantam team.

One of four girls trying out for goalie, Anika, skated up to Zoey. Smiling, she said, "You're so fast! I don't know where you get the energy."

Zoey didn't know what to say. So she said nothing.

"For someone so quiet," said Anika, "you really play hard."

Zoey listened as Coach Mikom began the skating drills in the corner. They had to skate around the circles painted on the ice. Once each girl completed the first circle, the next player would start. Zoey was in the middle of the line. She watched as the other girls took off, legs crossing over and blades cutting ice. Some girls were faster than others. But no one caught up to the girl in front of her.

Eager to prove herself, Zoey leaned into each curve. Her legs followed her core, all parts working together to go faster. By the third circle, the centre one, Zoey could see the black curls flowing from the helmet of the girl in front of her, Mel. Mel had shone in the first two tryouts. She was clearly the team's star.

Zoey saw Mel glance back, then pick up her pace. But so did Zoey. Zoey passed Mel on the way to the fourth circle.

"Show-off!" snarled Mel.

Zoey glided into the line along the boards and watched as Mel approached seconds later. *Hey!* thought Zoey as Mel nudged back ahead of Zoey instead of taking the place behind her in line.

Waiting behind Mel, Zoey admired Mel's top-of-the-line skates. Zoey knew they must have cost six-hundred bucks. Mel's shiny black one-piece stick was worth another two hundred. Add in a few hundred for the latest helmet and pants, and Zoey figured Mel had on close to fifteen-hundred dollars' worth of equipment. Even her gloves were brand new and bright pink. *And she calls* me *a show-off*, thought Zoey.

It was time for the two-on-ones. Coach Mikom had the forwards form two lines, one in each circle at one end. He had the defence line up along the boards at the far blue line. The forwards were supposed to skate up the ice, passing the puck. When they crossed the first blue line, a defender would skate to centre ice and begin skating backwards. The forwards had to find a good shot on net and try to score.

First up were Mel and Tia. Tia was another strong player and the Sharks' captain. The two moved up the ice swiftly, trading pin-point passes. Zoey admired their quick releases and soft cushioning of the puck. Tia took the defender wide and fired Mel a clear pass. Mel shot, but Anika made the save.

Then it was Zoey's turn. She told her partner to criss-cross in the opponent's end. They were facing Kat — the best defender on the ice. As she passed the blue line, Zoey skated the puck behind her partner. The other player crossed as well. Kat wasn't fooled. She stayed between the two forwards and blocked the passing lane. Zoey saw an opening. If she could feather a pass over Kat's stick, her partner would have an open corner. Zoey could send a saucer pass swirling through the air, like a flying saucer, to land flat on the ice. Zoey had to shoot on her backhand, and it was harder to saucer that way. But she had to try. With soft hands, Zoey lifted the puck over Kat's stick. It spun directly onto the stick of her partner, who easily sniped a goal into the open side of the net.

Zoey felt a tap on her back. Anika smiled and shook her head. "Nice pass, girl," she said. "Wayne Gretzky couldn't have done it any better."

A full face-mask couldn't hide the scowl on Mel's face.

The last challenge before scrimmage was a battle drill. Two players would start, one in each end circle. From opposite sides they raced around a pylon at centre ice. Then they skated back to be first to the puck and score. Zoey watched the other girls closely as she waited her turn.

Tia beat another player to the puck. She skated in free and found the five-hole — the empty space between a goalie's legs.

Kat won a close race and rang a slap shot off the crossbar.

Mel was supposed to battle another newbie, but Coach Mikom bumped Zoey up in line. Zoey was going to challenge the team's star player. Two seconds before the whistle, Mel jumped the gun and darted ahead. Zoey raced to catch up but Mel was moving fast. Zoey dug in her edges and extended her stride. She caught and tied up Mel just as she was going to shoot. The puck slid off into the corner of the ice.

Mel knocked Zoey's stick out of her hands. Zoey skated by and laughed. She knew it was wrong to taunt Mel. But she just couldn't help it.

Tryouts

For the scrimmage, Coach Mikom divided the team into two squads. Mel was on the Reds and Zoey was on the Blues. Zoey, a playmaker, set up two goals. Mel, a scorer, netted two on her own. The scrimmage ended in a tie.

Zoey left the ice feeling like she'd embarrassed herself.

2 Making THE CUT

Off the ice, Zoey felt like she didn't belong. In the change room she kept her head down and undressed quickly, hoping no one would talk to her. The sixty girls trying out were divided into two dressing rooms. Zoey was glad Mel wasn't in the same one she was in. But Anika was beside her.

"You sure got under Mel's skin today," said the goalie. "I saw her knock your stick out of your hands."

Zoey's gaze didn't leave her own skate laces. "Yeah, what's her problem?"

"Oh, Mel has always wanted all the attention," said Anika. "Her parents came here from Trinidad and started a chocolate business. They're crazy rich."

"Yeah, I could tell by her gear," said Zoey. "Nothing but the best."

Zoey didn't really need flashy skates or a fancy stick. But it was her dream to make the team. The truth was that Zoey didn't know how she'd pay the team fees if she did make it. Her parents had a small farm and they had always made just enough to keep it going. In the summer, Zoey's dad had hurt his back and was not able to work. So the Findleys were struggling even more these days.

Zoey was first out of the change room. She took a seat in the stands and hauled up her bag beside her. The final team list would be posted soon. Each minute felt like an hour to Zoey. She was starving and her stomach growled. She was tired and her thighs ached. She was nervous and she told herself that there was no way in the world she could crack the line-up of the mighty Barrie Sharks.

Finally the team trainer, Carla, came out to post the list on the board. Zoey waited for Carla to leave and walked up to the board slowly. *Well, this is it*, she thought. She scanned the list for her name. And there it was . . . Zoey Findley. For a moment, she feared that it was a list of the cuts, not the players who made the team. She double-checked the heading: Roster: Barrie Sharks Bantam Girls. Zoey had made it!

Coach Mikom stopped Zoey as she crossed the parking lot on her way to the bus stop. "Great work out there today, Zoey," he said. "You're some playmaker! I'm glad you'll be joining us this year." He handed her the team list with all the phone numbers, including his own.

Zoey nodded and mumbled thanks. She was pleased she had made the team. While she waited for the bus, she saw a giant chocolate-coloured Hummer race by. She could see Mel inside. It reminded Zoey that she had no idea how to raise the money to play.

Zoey was dying to tell her parents that she'd made the Barrie Sharks. She hadn't told them she'd been trying out. So it would come as a big surprise. But as she rode the bus home, she thought about waiting. She needed to figure out how to pay the fee of a thousand dollars. If she couldn't do it, there was no way she'd be able to play. Her family didn't have the cash for extras. It was especially true now, with money going to a worker to maintain the farm until her dad's back healed.

That night, Zoey twisted and turned. She couldn't get to sleep. There didn't seem to be an answer. She had no time for a part-time job, because she had to help out on the farm and keep up with her school work. She was happy to do her share. But there was no other place she could go for money. None of her friends had any money. And Zoey was too shy and proud to ask anyway.

Zoey needed a thousand bucks. And she needed it quick.

What Zoey needed was help. And the thought of asking anyone for it scared her to death. But she wanted to play for the Sharks more than anything. So she crept downstairs to the phone and called Anika.

"Wassup, newbie?" said the goalie.

Suddenly Zoey had a thought. Was it too late to call? "Ahh . . . never mind . . . I —" she choked.

"Spit it out, girl — we're teammates."

"Umm. You wouldn't know where someone could get . . . funding? I mean, to play hockey?"

There was silence. Zoey could feel she was turning red and was glad Anika couldn't see her.

"Oh, I remember now," said Anika at last. "A counsellor spoke to our class. There are programs out there . . . I don't remember the names, but I'm sure they're online."

Zoey thanked her and hung up. Back in bed, she decided that Monday after school she was going to the Innisfil Public Library. She was used to using the library to take out books and check her emails. She knew she could use a computer there to search for the programs. Plan in mind, Zoey fell asleep easily.

3 Finding THE FUNDS

The library was busy. Zoey had to wait twenty minutes for a computer to free up. She logged on and searched "hockey funding Ontario." This led to KidSport Ontario, which offered support to "under-resourced children playing organized sports." Kids under eighteen could be given up to $250 for fees and/or equipment. That was great, but not enough. So Zoey searched "hockey grants Canada." That brought up the Canadian Tire Jumpstart program. If Zoey could get the approval of the regional store manager, she could get up to $300 to play above house-league level. This was awesome, but still not enough. Zoey typed in "Barrie youth funding" and found the community youthreach program. They gave grants of $250.

Zoey leaned back and threw her hands in the air in frustration. The programs were generous. But they just didn't come close to covering the full costs of playing rep hockey. She wasn't even sure if you could combine them. But if you could, she would still be $200 short.

There was an hour before her dad was coming to pick her up. Rather than just sit there, Zoey filled in as much of the application forms as she could. She skipped the parts that asked for details of her family's income. She saved the digital forms and printed paper copies. But she was tempted to throw the copies away. What good would it do anyway?

By the time Zoey's dad arrived in his truck, all her hope was gone. She stared out the car window, silent and glum.

"What's wrong, Zoey?" asked her father. "You don't seem yourself."

"Dad, I . . . "

"You what, Zoey?"

"I hope you're not mad, but I tried out for the Barrie Sharks. And I made the cut!"

Her dad looked surprised. Then he smiled broadly. "Mad?" he said. "How could I be mad? I'm so happy for you."

"Don't get too excited, Dad. The fees are out of this world. I know we can't afford it. There are these funding programs, and I've filled in all the forms. But none of them give you enough. Even if I get them all, I still need two hundred dollars. I guess I'll just have to play on the outdoor rink for another year."

Her dad's brow furrowed.

"I'm sorry, Dad," Zoey said. "I know we're going through rough times."

"No, no, it's not that," he said. "Times are hard. I'm just amazed that you did all this on your own. You tried out and made the Sharks. You found and filled out the forms. It takes a lawyer to get those things. If you're that committed, I can fork out two hundred bucks. We're struggling, but we're not completely broke."

Zoey smiled. "That's great, Dad. But I don't know if you can get more than one grant at a time. And the Canadian Tire one needs special approval from a store manager."

"I don't see why you can't get that," said her dad. "You just have to explain your situation. And how could the Innisfil Canadian Tire turn down a young and promising Innisfil player?"

"I hope you're right," said Zoey.

The rusty truck pulled in to the farmhouse lane and came to a stop.

"By the way," said her father, "I'm proud of you."

"That's good. Because there's some financial stuff you're gonna have to give me to put in the applications."

Her father laughed. "No, problem."

"Thanks, Dad."

***

The next morning, Zoey's dad dug up the information Zoey needed. That afternoon, Zoey hurried to the library. She logged on to the computer, filled in the missing data and sent in the three forms. Leaving nothing to chance, she walked straight down the road to Canadian Tire and asked to speak to the store manager.

Zoey was so nervous her hands were shaking. She thought of running back out into the street before the manager answered the page. But she couldn't give up her dream because of some nerves.

The store manager, Mr. Davis, met her at the service desk.

Zoey introduced herself. Then she drew a deep breath and explained everything. At least Mr. Davis wasn't a stranger. He knew Zoey's father. And Zoey knew Mr. Davis's daughter Emily. Emily was one grade ahead of Zoey, now in high school.

Mr. Davis listened carefully. Then he said, "You know, my daughter plays soccer and basketball. Both have been so good for her. They've taught her teamwork, leadership skills and good sportsmanship."

"Emily's a great athlete," agreed Zoey. "I wish I could play soccer like her."

"Well, it sounds like you're quite the hockey player," he said. "Another Hayley Wickenheiser. I'll be happy to recommend that your rep request be approved. When it crosses my desk, I'll do everything I can to push it through."

Zoey smiled shyly. "Thanks, Mr. Davis."

"You can call me Tom," he said. "After all, we're

doing business here. When's your first game?"

"Two weeks from now," said Zoey. "But we have a couple of practices before that."

"I'll try to get the money to the Sharks by the first game," he said. "Go Sharks!"

Zoey asked to borrow the store phone and called her dad for a pick-up. While she waited, her hands finally stopped shaking, but her worries weren't over: she still desperately needed the grants from the KidSport and youthreach programs. Without this money, she knew she wouldn't be able to play.

4 Keep YOUR HEAD UP

Zoey was nervous about the first practice till she stepped onto the ice. As always, on the ice was where she felt she belonged.

After warm-up and stretches, Coach Mikom ran the girls through skating and passing drills. He had them kneel on one knee as he explained each drill on his whiteboard. The drills were skill-oriented and each player focused on their own work. So there was little chance for Zoey and Mel to get under each other's skin.

With thirty minutes left, the coach called everyone in. He divided the team for the scrimmage. As in the tryouts, Mel was placed on the Reds and Zoey the Blues. That scrimmage had ended in a tie. This time Zoey was looking forward to destroying Mel. She knew that the feeling wasn't the best model of teamwork or sportsmanship. But she didn't care. With Tia on Zoey's team, and Kat on Mel's, the two squads were balanced. Zoey felt her play could make the difference.

Anika skated to the Reds' net. Then she saw her mistake and skated back to the Blues' net. Zoey watched Anika pass by Mel and Kat. The goalie frowned and skated up to Zoey. "I don't know what's up," Anika told Zoey. "But keep your head up out there."

But Zoey was focused on the game. No drama was going to keep her from victory.

The puck dropped. Zoey swept it back to her defender, and Kat was on Zoey — like glue. Everywhere Zoey skated, Kat followed. It didn't matter if Zoey had the puck or not. Kat was her shadow. But a mean shadow, holding and hooking and hacking away.

When Zoey got back to the bench, Tia leaned towards her. "It looks like Mel and Kat are giving you the special treatment," Tia said. "They did the same thing to me when I joined the team. They tried to make it hard for me."

"Why?" asked Zoey.

"I don't know. Jealousy, I guess."

"What did you do?" Zoey asked.

"I fought through it," said Tia.

On their next shift, Tia won the race to a free puck and crossed the blue line. Zoey was with Tia on the wing. But Kat was all over Zoey, tying her up. With no one to pass to, Tia shot a wrist shot at the net. The puck rebounded off the goalie's pads. Zoey wrestled to break through Kat's hold. She got to the puck and lifted it over the fallen goalie's pad.

"That's the way, Zoey," said Tia. "Nice goal."

Zoey heard Mel tell Kat, "You'll have to do a lot better than that."

Zoey won the faceoff again, and drew the puck back to Marika. Marika passed it back. As the puck hit Zoey's stick, Kat used her foot to knock out Zoey's legs while pushing on her chest — a slew-foot. Zoey crashed to the ice. Mel picked up the loose puck. She raced down the wing and sniped a wrist shot into the top corner.

Mel and Kat tapped gloves. "That's more like it," said Mel.

On the bench, Zoey rubbed her sore back.

The Reds' second line pushed hard in the Blues' end. The centre blasted a slap shot from the circle. The puck missed the net. It rimmed around the boards out to the Blues forwards, giving them a fast break. But the Reds defenders broke it up.

Zoey was worried. She was new to the team. Could she still be cut if her play wasn't up to par? She had won every faceoff. But she hadn't done much since her first goal. Now the game was tied. Zoey knew she could make a difference by scoring the winning goal.

Zoey jumped the boards and stole the puck before Kat could blanket her. Kat recovered fast. She closed the gap as Zoey came across the blue line. Zoey faked left and cut right for a breakaway. Kat glanced to the bench and saw Coach Mikom talking to Carla. Seeing that they weren't watching, Kat reached with her stick blade and tripped Zoey. Zoey fell. Kat retrieved the puck and fired a long pass up the ice to Mel.

Coach Mikom looked up to see Mel deke around Anika to score the winning goal. "Sweet move, Mel!" he called. "Two laps, everyone, before you call it a night!"

Mel raced off with Kat.

For the first time since she had started to skate with the Barrie Sharks, Zoey lagged behind. She was floored by the loss. And she knew that the coach hadn't seen the penalties.

In the change room, Zoey kept to herself. But she watched as Anika confronted Kat. "That was pretty cheap," Anika said. "I guess it's the only way you can stop Zoey, eh?"

"I was going for the puck," said Kat.

"Yeah," said Mel. "Kat can't help it if Zoey stepped on her blade."

"Yeah, right," said Anika, pursing her lips. "That's no way to win."

Mel glared at Zoey. "Whine all you want, Zoey. It won't change anything."

"Zoey's not whining," said Tia. "She didn't say a word."

Mel ignored the captain and turned to Kat. "So I'll pick you up Friday night?"

"Okay!" said Kat. "What should I bring?" It was like the rest of the team didn't exist.

"Just your skis and a bathing suit."

"I can't wait to see your chalet."

"I can't wait to try out our new hot tub."

Kat sighed. "It'll feel so nice after a day on the slopes."

"You don't know the half of it," said Mel. "My mom has a Swedish masseuse coming over. We can have massages."

Zoey changed quickly. She didn't know what she hated more: losing the scrimmage, or hearing about Mel and Kat's bestie winter retreat.

"Good practice, Zoey!" said Anika.

"Not really," said Zoey. "But thanks."

Anika smiled. "All you needed was a referee."

Zoey zipped up her hockey bag. She was first out of the room.

Coach Mikom stopped her in the hall. "What happened out there? You looked pretty shook up."

Zoey wanted to tell him. But she couldn't find the words. And she didn't want her first practice with the team to end with her snitching. She stared at Coach Mikom blankly.

"Hockey's a tough game," he said.

Zoey shrugged.

"You know, when I was young, I was a pretty good player. I left the Rez to play on the Barrie Colts. A lot of people didn't want me there. They tried to make it really hard for me."

"What did you do?" asked Zoey.

"I tried hard. I played well. My efforts couldn't be denied."

So Coach saw more than it looked like, thought Zoey. Still, she didn't know what to say. Sometimes trying hard just wasn't enough.

"Don't worry," Coach Mikom said. "I see the fire in your eyes when you play. You'll be okay."

Zoey hoped he was right.

5 First-Line CENTRE

The big day had finally come. After school was the first game of the season. Zoey wanted the day to pass quickly so she could play. But she had yet to hear back from KidSport Ontario and Barrie youthreach. True to his word, Mr. Davis had rushed the JumpStart application and the team had already received that funding. And she had handed in the $200 her dad had scrounged together. But Coach Mikom had told all his players to pay their fees by the first game. Zoey had only paid half. What if he didn't let her play until she paid the rest? What if he cut her from the team?

Zoey headed downstairs to the kitchen.

Her mom passed her toast with peanut butter. "Have you got a ride to the game tonight?"

"Yeah," said Zoey. "I asked Anika and her dad is driving. He'll pick me up here at four-fifteen."

"Good," said her mom. "Dad's sorry he can't drive. We can't afford the gas . . . not when there are so many away games."

"It's okay," said Zoey.

"When his back's a little better, we'll come to a home game."

A part of Zoey was glad her parents couldn't come. As much as she loved them, their farmers' clothes and small-town ways made her cringe.

★★★

After a school day that seemed to last for weeks, Zoey went to the library. She hadn't been able to focus on her schoolwork. She spent English worrying that she'd filled out her applications wrong. During Math she feared they wouldn't be approved.

Zoey hurried to the computer and logged in to her email. There they were. Letters from the KidSport and youthreach programs. Both could be combined with other funding. Both were approved.

Zoey couldn't believe it. She reread the messages slowly. It was true. She had received enough in grants to cover the registration fee for rep hockey.

Zoey ran to the truck when her father came to take her home.

"Dad, the funding came through — all of it!" Zoey read him the emails.

"That's wonderful," her dad beamed. "I'm so proud of you."

"They're sending the cheques to the Sharks," she said.

"That's awesome," he said. "We'd better get home. You have chicken pasta to eat. And your ride will be arriving soon."

Back at the house, Zoey wolfed down her game-day meal. She checked her equipment bag to make sure she had everything.

"Wow, does that stuff stink!" said her father.

"Yeah," nodded Zoey. "I think I'm gonna have to air it out more often."

"Preferably not in the kitchen."

Zoey laughed. She put on her winter jacket and boots. As she waited by the front door, she watched out the window to see when her drive arrived. With no money to offer for gas, she sure didn't want to keep Anika's father waiting.

A silver mini-van pulled into the lane. Zoey ran out and reached to open the side door but it opened by itself. Next to the shiny van, her dad's rusted truck looked like junkyard scrap. Zoey couldn't help but feel embarrassed. She sat beside Anika while her dad sat up front like a chauffeur.

"How long have you been playing hockey?" Anika asked Zoey as she settled in.

"Six years," said Zoey.

"Wow, you got good quick."

"How long have you been playing?"

"Since I was three," said Anika. "My dad had only been in Canada for five years. He wanted to do everything Canadians do and he fell in love with hockey. At first I played just to be with him and make him happy. But then I started to love the game, too. Now I couldn't live without it."

Anika's dad glanced back at Zoey. "I coached Anika's team one year when she played tyke. We only lost one game that season. And we won the championship. Not bad coaching for a cricket-loving immigrant, eh?"

"That's awesome," said Zoey.

"I think it was the team, Dad, not you," said Anika.

"No, no, the coaching was superb," said Anika's dad. "I picked out the best drills and got the girls working as a team."

"If you say so, Dad," said Anika.

"I've always wanted to try cricket," said Zoey. "It looks like so much fun."

"It is," said Anika. "This summer you can come over and I'll teach you."

"I'd like that," said Zoey, as the van pulled into the arena parking lot.

The Sharks were playing against the Etobicoke Dolphins. Zoey followed Anika into the Centennial Park Arena. It was huge. When they passed the food stand, Zoey saw nachos, pizza and pretzels. Not just burgers and fries. Anika bought a blue sports drink for after the game. Zoey had to settle for tap water.

Carla met them at the door to the change room.

She held out a white cloth bag. "Cell phones in here, girls — please," she said. "Coach Mikom doesn't want you distracted while you're getting ready to play."

Anika put her phone into the bag and took a seat. Head down, Zoey walked past Carla.

"Zoey, your phone needs to go in here," said the trainer.

Zoey looked up. Her face was red. "I don't have one," she said.

"Oh, I'm sorry," said Carla. "Carry on."

"No cell phone? Are you living in the Dark Ages?" teased Mel.

Zoey sat between Anika and Tia, across from Mel.

Mel went on. "I always get the new smart phone the day it comes out."

Tia and Anika ignored her. "It's nice to go un-plugged sometimes," said Tia to Zoey. "You must have a lot of extra time in your day."

Zoey smiled and nodded. She dressed quickly. She wanted to be ready for Coach Mikom's pre-game talk.

Skates tied, Zoey put on her shoulder pads. The cell phone insult had just faded in her mind when Mel crossed the room towards her.

"Where did you get this junk?" Mel asked, glaring. "Your long johns have holes in them. One of your shin pads is cracked. Your shoulder pads look like they come from the last century."

Zoey didn't want to admit where her gear came

from. She borrowed half of it from her dad. She had picked up the other half from a second-hand sports store.

"Hey, those old-school shoulder-pads were good enough for Bobby Orr," said Anika. "I think Zoey's retro cool."

Mel went back to her seat. Zoey pulled on her jersey as Coach Mikom came in. *It was a lot nicer during tryouts*, she thought, *when Mel was in a different dressing room.*

Coach Mikom told the girls that they had worked hard during the tryouts and practices. That they were ready to show the Dolphins what the Sharks were made of. He reminded them to support the puck and move it quickly. He told them to play as a team. Then he announced the starting line-up: "Anika in goal. Marika and Kat on D. Mel and Jan on the wing, and Zoey, centre. Second line: Tia between Winnie and Sue. Niki and Emily on defence. And last but not least: Haya, Alice and Trisha, with Val and Allie."

Zoey was surprised. She was a rookie. She didn't expect to be named first-line centre.

Anika patted Zoey's back with her glove.

Tia winked. "Congrats, Zoey. You earned it!"

"But I'm the centre," argued Mel. "I always have been."

"Yes, and you've done well," said Coach Mikom. "But Zoey is strong on faceoffs. She wins more than eighty-per cent. And she's a great playmaker. I need you on the wing scoring goals."

Coach Mikom headed out to the bench. Carla and the girls followed.

On the way, Zoey saw Mel turn to Jan and Kat. "This is a big mistake. My dad raises a lot of money for this team. We need to do whatever it takes to win. So whatever you do, don't pass to Zoey."

Zoey was about to protest when Mel turned to her and snarled, "Girl, do you have some sort of gland problem? 'Cause you stink. If you want to sit on the same bench as me, you'd better get your gear washed."

As Zoey stepped onto the ice for the warm-up, she thought about what Mel had said. Mel's insults hurt. But surely Zoey's linemates would pass to her. How could the line succeed if they didn't?

6 SHUNNED

Zoey lost the opening faceoff. The Dolphins centre shifted forward and tied up her stick. The Dolphins winger raced in to pick up the loose puck.

Mel skated by Zoey. "Nice draw!" she hooted. "This is working out well."

No one ever used that faceoff move back on the outdoor rink, thought Zoey. She'd have to work on it.

Mel chased down the winger and stole back the puck. She sped down the wing. She passed it to Jan and Jan passed it back. Zoey had kept up with the play and was clear in the slot. Mel glanced Zoey's way. Then she took a bad angle shot on goal.

The Dolphins goalie made the easy save.

On their shifts, the Sharks' second and third lines fought the Dolphins to a stand-still.

Zoey jumped the boards. This was the shift to make a difference. Mel and Jan had made their point. They would pass to her now.

Marika had the puck behind the Sharks' net. Zoey

skated to the hash-marks — two lines on the faceoff circle by the boards — and Marika put the puck on her stick. Zoey was glad to see that at least one teammate was acting sanely.

Zoey skated to the open ice. Mel joined her on the rush. Zoey gave the puck to Mel and rushed the net. Zoey was clear again. She called and called, but this time Mel didn't even look. She cut inside. The Dolphins defender reached out with her stick and poke-checked the puck away from her.

Zoey hoped that Tia's line could break the stalemate. Tia hit the ice. Dreadlocks swaying, Tia powered down the wing. She ripped a rocket off the left goalpost. It was the closest the Sharks had come to scoring.

Near the end of the first period, Kat caught Mel with a fast-break pass. It gave the Sharks a three-on-one. Mel and Jan fed the puck back and forth. Zoey called and waited on the open side for the cross-pass, but they ignored her. Soon the two girls were too deep in the Dolphins' end to make anything happen.

With two Sharks stranded in the corner, the Dolphins raced back up-ice. Zoey skated hard on the back-check to try and catch and stop her opponents. But she couldn't break up the play. With pinpoint passing, the Dolphins worked Anika out of position. The winger tapped a pass into the open net.

In a fury, Zoey forgot how expensive hockey sticks were. She broke hers over the crossbar. Then she skated to Mel and Jan. "What's wrong with you two?" she demanded. "I was completely open!"

"Temper, temper, Zoey," said Mel. "You've got to calm down."

Anika argued, "Girls, all you had to do was pass it to Zoey. She had a clear break."

Mel and Jan just skated away, shaking their heads.

Zoey skated to the bench. She regretted her tantrum. New sticks didn't grow on trees. *But if it makes them see how important passing is*, she thought, *it's worth it.*

In the second period, the Sharks fell apart. With Mel and Jan still not passing to Zoey, it was as if the team was a player short. The Sharks' rushes were easily broken up, and the Dolphins began to control the play. Halfway through the second period, the Dolphins scored two quick goals. The Sharks ended the period down 3–0.

In the change room, the Sharks sat silent with their heads down.

Coach Mikom tried to rally the team. "Some of you are playing selfishly. It's killing us. Hockey's a team sport. A team can only win when all of its members are playing together and working as one." He turned to his two first-line wingers. "Mel! Jan! I don't know why, but you're not seeing Zoey out there. Take a look and send her some passes. She's been open all game. We can do this, girls! Now get out there and play like a team."

Zoey hoped it wasn't too late for the game to get back on track.

Shunned

Anika and Tia led the team onto the ice. Anika took her place in goal and Tia skated to the bench.

Zoey won the faceoff and sent Mel a quick pass. Then she skated wide into the open ice and called for the puck. Mel drew her stick back. With all her strength, she rifled a pass to Zoey. Zoey wasn't prepared for the pepper. The puck blasted through her blade.

"What's wrong, hotshot?" said Mel. "Can't handle a pass?"

But no one could have handled that bullet, thought Zoey.

Next shift, Zoey found herself alone deep in the slot — the area in front of the goalie between the two faceoff circles. If Jan could feed her the puck, Zoey would have a quick clear shot. But Jan fired a rocket that Zoey couldn't settle. It was a golden chance missed. No, it was worse. It was a sure goal ruined.

Tia's line had taken Coach Mikom's advice and were passing smoothly. But the Dolphins goalie was strong. She stopped all their chances. The Sharks' third line, centred by Haya, grinded hard. But they couldn't get near the Dolphins' goal.

Zoey noticed that no one covered her teammates to the side of the net. She planted herself there and called for the puck as Mel looked to shoot. It was the perfect chance for a low hard pass that Zoey could redirect. But Mel took aim and blasted a high hard slap shot that hit Zoey's thigh. It hurt!

Down by three with five minutes left, the Sharks panicked. Each of them tried to do it all on their own. Mel stickhandled through two Dolphins players. But she was stopped by the last defender. Jan and Zoey had been with her, but Mel wasn't looking to pass.

As Zoey rushed down the wing she saw Jan in scoring position. But Zoey kept the puck and missed with a low-percentage shot. Even Marika joined in, mounting an end-to-end rush. But she shot the puck wide and put herself out of position. The Dolphins broke back out quickly. They scored their fourth and final goal with a beautiful two-on-one.

Coach Mikom slammed his clipboard against the bench. Zoey was shocked. Coach Mikom had seemed calm and reasonable. But he was clearly competitive and feeling frustrated. In the change room, he told the girls again that they had to play as a team if they wanted to win. "I don't know what happened out there. We weren't passing. We weren't looking for the open player. When we did start passing, nobody could pick up the passes. And then everybody tried to play the hero." He shook his head. "But it's only our first game. I have faith in you girls. I know what you're capable of. With a little work we'll turn this around."

Zoey wasn't as sure as her coach. She didn't want to believe it, but it looked like Mel had fired a slap shot at her on purpose. That just wasn't teamwork.

7 Arch RIVALS

The first home game for the Sharks was against the Brampton Canadettes. Tia led the warm-up run. They sped around the inside of the arena and up and down the stairs in the stands. Mel and Kat stayed on the team captain's tail, with Anika and Zoey close behind. The rest of the team followed in a long line.

Back in the dressing room, Tia led stretches. She turned on the team's playlist. The music was a mix of hip-hop, pop, rock, country and soul. Anika told Zoey that last year's players had let her know their favourite tunes. She asked for Zoey's. Zoey told her that anything by Drake got her going.

Zoey followed the team stretches. She worked her ankles, knees, hips, back, neck and shoulders. Her body was feeling loose. But she couldn't get the last game out of her head. No one but Marika had passed her the puck. Mel had tried to take off her head with a slap shot. Zoey wanted to confront Mel. But she was too shy and too worried about creating team drama.

Maybe the coach's speeches had hit a nerve and this time the Sharks would play as a team.

In shin-pads, socks and hockey pants, Zoey and Tia stepped into the hall. They passed a golf ball between them with their sticks.

"Brampton and the Sharks go back a long way," said Tia. "They always beat us."

"They must be good," said Zoey. She stick-handled the ball smoothly and rapidly before passing it back.

"Yeah, the games are close," said Tia. "But the Canadettes are tough and fast. They've got this one defender, Ting Chang. She's a beast out there. Keep an eye out for her."

"What number is she?" asked Zoey.

"I don't know," said Tia. "But you'll find out soon enough."

Zoey skated to centre-ice and waited for the ref for the faceoff. At the blue line, the Brampton defence partners were staring at her. The big one seemed to be asking questions that the small one answered. The big one had broad shoulders and muscular thighs. Zoey could see her scowl from the red line. Her stick looked twice the length of her partner's. Straight, jet-black hair flowed out of her helmet and down her shoulders and back.

The puck dropped. Zoey snatched it back to Kat. Kat moved it to Marika. Marika passed it up to Mel. Mel crossed the red line and gave it to Zoey. Zoey hit the blue line and returned it to Mel.

This is promising, thought Zoey, as she entered scoring position. She called for the puck. Mel glanced over but opted to shoot instead of pass. The goalie made an easy glove save and the whistle blew.

As Zoey skated by the goalie, she felt a sharp slash to her calf.

"You don't belong here," chirped the big Brampton defender. "Get back to the farm."

This must be Ting, thought Zoey. Somehow word had gotten around. Maybe the smaller defender had told Ting where Zoey was from. Zoey had no idea where that pipsqueak would have learned her background. All she knew for sure was that that slash was dirty. Her leg was throbbing.

Brampton penned Tia's line in the Sharks' end. The Canadettes were big and moved the puck well. The defence pinched every chance they got, pouncing on the puck deep in the offensive zone.

The Sharks' third line forced a turnover. Haya almost jammed a loose puck in.

Midway through the first period, Ting led a rush for Brampton. She blasted a slap shot into the top corner. Skating by Zoey, she snarled, "I guess it's back to the outdoor rink and frozen cow dung pucks for you."

Zoey was about to chirp back, but she held her tongue. She thought that winning was the best form of revenge. She joined the rush with Mel and Jan. The three girls passed well from blue line to blue line. But once they hit the offensive zone, Mel and Jan kept the puck to themselves. Zoey could see what was going on. Her linemates were passing enough so Coach Mikom could see. But they were saving the real scoring chances for each other.

Zoey was furious. Ting was slashing and chirping her every shift. Her own teammates were holding her back. It would have been easy to give up. But Zoey recalled what Coach Mikom had told her. He'd tried so hard that his efforts couldn't be denied. Zoey knew she could work even harder. She also decided to get even with Ting.

Deep in the second period, Zoey picked up speed. She skated in on the big Brampton defender. There was room to go wide. But Zoey didn't want to just get by Ting. She wanted to make Ting look foolish. Zoey reached forward with her stick, rolled her wrists, and drew the puck back to her left foot. She pushed the puck to her right side and sped up, protecting the puck with her leg. It was a classic toe-drag. In an instant she was past Ting. Her flat-footed opponent was left poking where the puck used to be. Zoey had a clear break. Her shot found the five-hole to tie the game.

Zoey, with a smile, skated towards Ting. Ting's face flushed red with shame and rage.

As Ting passed, she elbowed Zoey in the head.

Zoey doubled over. Coach Mikom yelled from the bench, "Hey, what was that?"

As Zoey was led back to the bench, Tia skated in. She cross-checked Ting. The big defender stumbled forward but did not fall. Ting turned back and cocked her arm to pummel Tia. But the ref grabbed the defender before she could land a blow.

Both Ting and Tia were given penalties. Zoey wanted to go back out. But Carla had her sit out the rest of the second period to be safe.

The third period was hard fought and the game ended a tie.

Coach Mikom told the girls that they'd played well. "The Canadettes are a strong team and we battled them to a draw. There's no shame in that. By the play-offs, I think we'll have them."

As usual, Zoey changed quickly. But this time she didn't leave right away. She waited for Tia and walked out with her. "Thanks for jumping in," she told the team captain. "Ting is a piece of work."

"No problem," replied Tia. "I'm just lucky the ref grabbed her in time! Otherwise, I'd be on my way to the hospital."

"Or the cemetery," said Zoey. "I can't say you didn't warn me."

Tia smiled. "Do you need a ride?"

"I'm good. I take the bus."

"Don't be silly! My dad will give you a lift. He loves carting my friends all over the place."

Zoey laughed. "Great then. Let's make him happy.

By the way, I love your dreadlocks. I wish I could do that with my hair."

"Hey, you've got beautiful hair. And probably easier. It takes me an hour each morning to get this mess under control."

The girls found Tia's dad in the lobby and headed out to the car.

Halfway home, Zoey realized that Tia hadn't been kidding. Her dad was delighted to be driving miles out of his way to drop off a stranger. "Are you excited about the tournament?" he asked Zoey. "I know I am."

"Yes," said Zoey. But Zoey was hiding something. The Burlington Splash tournament cost an extra seventy dollars per player to register. Plus the Sharks were staying in a nice hotel to save time and to let the team bond. Zoey couldn't afford any of that.

8 Getting TO THE SPLASH

Zoey didn't know what to do. She'd already used up the available funding programs. And her dad had given all he could. The only option seemed to be to pull out of the tournament. She would call Coach Mikom the day before they left and tell him she was sick. That way she could keep playing the regular games that her paid registration covered. But there was another tournament later in the year, and she'd have to fake sickness again. And she was dying to play. And the team needed her, even if her linemates didn't know it.

The next morning, while gobbling her breakfast, Zoey got an idea. She thought about how the local boys' baseball league got sponsors to pay for each team's jerseys. Some summer evenings she would catch a baseball game with her mom and dad. Baseball was fun, but there was lots of down-time. Zoey would read the names of the sponsors on the backs of the jerseys. She could only remember one: Lopez's Windows and Doors. She didn't know if they funded sports things other than jerseys. And she was scared to ask for money. Going to Canadian Tire had been hard enough, but at least they expected requests. Approaching a business and begging for cash was a whole different thing. But Zoey knew it had to be done.

Lopez's was several line roads over. So after school Zoey had her father drive.

"Dad, I'm scared," she said. "Will you come in with me?"

"Zoey," he said. "I think this is something you've got to do on your own. Just be yourself."

"Yeah, I guess so," said Zoey. She'd been practising her pitch all day. She went over it one last time in her head as she entered the building.

"What can I do for you?" said the woman at the desk. She was wearing a white blouse and silver earrings. She smelled like lilacs.

"I'd like to ask Mr. Lopez to sponsor me," said Zoey. "I know he helped out the boys' baseball league. I play hockey . . . girls' hockey."

"Good for you!" said the woman. "I'll ring him and let him know you're here. But I should warn you, he's only ever sponsored boys' baseball. His two sons play — they're very good. But it can't hurt to ask, can it now?"

Zoey nodded. On the wall behind the reception desk were several photos of little league teams. The store name was on all the jerseys. The woman was right — just baseball.

Mr. Lopez was a large bearded man who wore his sleeves rolled up. He came out to greet Zoey. "What can I do for you young lady?"

Zoey explained everything. "So," she said at the end, "I raised the money to cover the basic fees. But tournaments are extra and I need more money to cover my share of those fees and hotel bills."

"How much more?" Mr. Lopez asked.

"Five-hundred dollars," said Zoey. That would cover both tournaments the team was signed up for.

"Well you know, Zoey, I've watched the Canadian women's hockey team play many times. The games are exciting. All those great players, well, they make me proud. I'll do it! Who should I make the cheque out to?"

"Zoey Findley," Zoey said, relieved. "Thank you so much."

"It's my pleasure. Maybe I'll see you in the Olympics some day!"

Zoey smiled. "It'd be a dream come true."

"Just one thing," said Mr. Lopez. "Make sure you bring me a hockey picture — of you. I'd like to put it up on the wall with all the baseball teams. Zoey . . . and the boys of summer."

Zoey promised she would do just that. Then she waited while the receptionist wrote out a cheque for Mr. Lopez to sign.

The Playmaker

***

Zoey got a ride to the tournament with Anika's parents. She had enough money to cover her hotel room and meals. But she didn't want her parents to have to pay their own expenses. Besides, Dad's back was worse and he had to stay in bed for the weekend.

The drive was fun. After a good chat, each girl dug out a *Harry Potter* book. When they found out they both loved tales of magic and adventure, Anika suggested that Zoey read the *Tales of the Panchatantra*, the oldest surviving fables of India. Zoey told Anika to read *The High Deeds of Finn MacCool*.

Reading made the time pass quickly. Before she knew it, Zoey was standing in the hotel lobby. She gawked at the ornate rug, the marble pillars, the leather chairs and red sofas. She'd never seen such luxury, never mind stayed in a place that grand.

Anika's dad checked in his family and helped Zoey do the same. Zoey was given a room next to the suite Anika was sharing with her parents. All the Sharks were on the same floor, except Mel, whose father had booked the penthouse suite.

It took several swipes for Zoey to open her door with the plastic key card. She dumped her hockey bag in the corner and threw herself onto the queen-sized bed. After snuggling the pillows, she jumped up and checked out the mini-bar, microwave, coffee maker and big-screen TV. Everything was shiny and new.

There was a knock on her door. It was Anika with a bowl of green grapes. The two girls watched the second period of the Leafs game. Then, with an hour to curfew and an early game the next morning, Anika called it a night. She headed next door to her room.

Zoey put on her pyjamas. She settled under the covers to read more *Harry Potter.*

In the quiet of her own hotel room, Zoey could hear the phone ring next door in Anika's room. Zoey felt guilty listening in. But the walls were so thin it couldn't be helped.

"Hi, Mel," Zoey heard Anika say. "Yeah, I know the Leafs are playing. I watched the second period."

Silence, then Anika said, "Who's all there? . . . Great, I'll be right up. But I have to be back by curfew . . . Yeah, I know, everyone does."

Zoey heard the door open. She waited for Anika's knock on her door, but it never came. She waited five minutes for Mel to call and invite her up. But that didn't happen either. Zoey called Tia. Tia's father told her that Tia was watching the Leafs game in Mel's room with the other girls. Zoey waited another five minutes and called Mel.

"Hello," said Mel.

"Hi, it's Zoey. I hear you've got the Leafs —"

Zoey heard the phone click. Mel had hung up.

Zoey didn't know what to do. She couldn't believe

that Anika and Tia had left her behind. And she didn't want to believe that Mel had hung up on her, even though it was clear she did. Zoey felt sad and alone. But she didn't want to embarrass herself and crash the party.

Zoey turned out her light. She couldn't sleep, knowing she'd been rejected. Maybe joining the Sharks was the wrong decision, she thought. Who am I to think that I could fit in?

There was a knock on the door.

Zoey slipped out of bed and looked through the eye-hole. Anika, Tia and Marika were standing in the hallway outside her room.

"Open up, loser," said Anika, laughing.

As Zoey let the girls in, Tia handed her a slice of pizza off the plate in her hand. Zoey turned on the third period and the girls climbed on her bed.

"Why aren't you at Mel's watching the game?" asked Zoey. "With the rest of the team."

"We were," said Anika. "When I got there, I asked where you were because Mel had told me everyone was there. She said she didn't know or care! I didn't like that. So I grabbed Tia and Marika and a few slices of pizza. We decided to come down and watch the game with you."

"I called Mel and she hung up," said Zoey.

"If it makes you feel any better, only half the team was there." Tia was talking around a mouthful of pizza.

"The half that Mel likes right now."

"I can't believe Mel," said Zoey. "I'm gonna have to talk to her tomorrow, before the game. But not about this. I've got other things on my mind."

"What things?" asked Marika.

"Hockey things," said Zoey.

The Leafs game ended and Tia said she had to rush back to her room.

"But it's fifteen minutes till curfew," said Zoey. "We can hang for a while."

"It's not that," said Tia. "My mom's calling to make sure I got here okay. She's in Jamaica for the week helping my grandma."

Zoey said goodnight to her friends. She got under the covers and lay awake. What was she going to say to Mel?

9 HOCKEY DAD

Zoey waited in the lobby of the Appleby Ice Centre. She felt anxious. The thought of talking to Mel made her more nervous than asking Mr. Lopez for money. She saw Mel come in and crossed the room to confront her.

"We need to talk," said Zoey.

"Oh, sorry about last night," said Mel. "We got disconnected. I tried to call back but the phones at the hotel are messed."

"Forget about that," said Zoey. "It's about our line."

"What about it?" asked Mel.

"I may be crazy. But I want to win this tournament. Do you?"

"Of course I do," said Mel.

"Well, it's like Coach Mikom said. The only way we're gonna win is if we play as a team. You have to pass. Now I know that for some reason you don't like me. To be honest, I don't much like you, either. But we play on the same line. We've got to work together."

"I've been passing to you lots," said Mel, pouting.

"Only in the neutral zone. You know that when we have a scoring chance, you save it for yourself."

"That's not true. Did you ever think that maybe you should pass to me more often? I'm the goal scorer. You're the one who's supposed to be Little Miss Playmaker."

Wow, Mel must think we're all here just to make her look good, thought Zoey. "Look, we don't have to be friends. But there's no way we can win this thing — or the league championship — if even one of us plays selfishly."

Mel shrugged. She hurried off, pulling her hockey bag behind her.

The Sharks' early game was against the Stoney Creek Sabres. Zoey felt better for talking to Mel. But she wasn't hopeful that her message had gotten through.

The Sabres were a fast-skating team. Two of their players could stick-handle through opponents like they were pylons. It was all the Sharks could do just to keep up. *They must be early-birds*, thought Zoey, pumping her legs on a back-check.

Early in the game, Zoey didn't get any passes from Mel. Later, Mel threw her a few in the neutral zone. Near the end of the first period, Mel finally set up Zoey in the slot. But the goalie made a last-second kick save.

After the one good pass, Mel stopped passing again. It was as if she had tried passing to Zoey and seen that it didn't work. So she went back to ignoring her.

Halfway in, the two Sabres stars scored on a beautiful give-and-go play. The centre passed the puck to the winger and skated ahead. The winger passed the puck back, and the centre found the top corner of the net. Minutes later, Mel tried to skate end-to-end. But she lost the puck at the Sabres' blue line. The Stoney Creek centre split between the two defenders and lifted a backhand shot high up into the top of the net.

With seconds left in the second period, Zoey was open at the side of the net. Zoey knew Mel could see her. But Mel chose to shoot from a bad angle and missed the net.

With the Sharks down 2–0 in the third period, Zoey lost all hope. But then a surprising thing occurred. Mel started passing the puck to Zoey. Zoey was so shocked she missed the first pass. But she picked up the ones that followed. *Well, Mel must want to win after all*, thought Zoey. Zoey had realized that she wasn't giving Mel many chances. So she started passing back, and they both started including Jan. Soon the three girls were controlling the play and their line was getting lots of chances.

With seven minutes left, four perfect passes that travelled tape-to-tape paid off. Mel scored with a quick-release snap shot.

"Yeah! That's what I'm talking about!" shouted Coach Mikom from the bench.

With three minutes left, Mel slid a pass between a Sabres defender's legs and onto Zoey's stick-blade. Zoey lifted the puck over the goalie's pads for a second goal for the Sharks.

And with one minute left, Zoey returned the favour. She fed Mel a pass in the slot. Mel knocked it in to score the winning goal.

The Barrie Sharks had won their first game.

Zoey skated by for a fist pump, but Mel wouldn't raise her hand. "Don't think this makes us friends," Mel snarled.

Zoey didn't care. She needed linemates who would pass, not a new BFF.

★★★

The Sharks' second game was against the Aurora Panthers. The Panthers had been the best team in the division for the past two seasons. The Sharks were pleased to have won their first game. But they had to win the second as well to advance to the quarter-finals.

Skating to centre-ice, Zoey was surprised to hear a voice shouting her name from the stands. It was a voice she knew as well as her own. Standing behind the top railing was her father. He was screaming, "Go, Zoeeeeeey, go! Go, Zoeeeeeey, go!"

What was he doing there? Zoey knew he didn't have the money for the extra gas and meals. And the day before he'd been laid up in bed with an aching back. He was dressed in his work clothes: blue denim overalls, a red and black tartan lumberjack shirt and his favourite Maple Leafs cap. Zoey looked away quickly. She didn't want him to think that she liked his being there and making a lot of noise.

Zoey was embarrassed by her dad being there, but she played well. In the first period, she set up behind the Panthers' net. She fed the puck to Mel, who one-timed a shot over the goalie's blocker. Zoey's dad howled, "Whew-wee" and "Way to go, Sharks!" Zoey could hear that his voice sounded slurred. It was weird. At home her dad was soft-spoken and she'd never heard him yell.

The Panthers replied to the Sharks goal with two quick ones of their own.

In the second period, the Panthers added another two. But then Zoey sent a pass through two opponents right onto Mel's stick for the tip-in. Her dad jumped up and down yelling, "You can do it, Sharks!" His voice still sounded strange.

Things got rough for Zoey in the third period. The Panthers centre had lost most faceoffs all game, so she ran over Zoey to steal one and tripped her to win another. The young ref ignored both penalties.

Zoey's dad threw his arms in the air. "Are you blind, ref?" he shouted. "There's a game being played and you're missing it!"

The missed call ended in a fifth Panthers goal.

"Ref, you're killing us!" roared Zoey's dad.

The Sharks lost five to two. They were out of the tournament.

As the players left the ice, Zoey's dad ran down to the first level of seats. He stood just above the rink door the ref was exiting through. "I hope you know that you cost us the game," he said. "You should be ashamed of yourself." Zoey noticed he was having trouble with the "s" and "sh" sounds.

Zoey watched as the referee ignored the abuse and headed to her dressing room. But several well-dressed parents looked disgusted at her father's behaviour.

Kat's dad came to the ref's defence. "Shut up, you drunken bum," he said to Zoey's dad. "She's just a kid herself."

Zoey could see why the other parents looked down on her dad. But calling him that just didn't make sense. Her dad might have acted like a rude hockey dad, but he rarely drank. He couldn't be drunk. Zoey knew there must be some explanation. But she wasn't sure what it could be.

In the dressing room, Coach Mikom praised the great teamwork they showed on the ice.

Zoey and Anika walked out to the lobby, where Kat was waiting. Kat stormed over and pointed her finger at Zoey. "You know, you and your obnoxious dad are hurting this team. You really should quit."

Zoey wanted to defend her father. But she was too sad and confused to even try.

"Don't listen to her, Zoey," said Anika. "The Sharks need you."

After that weird game, Zoey wasn't sure who was right.

10 Over THE LINE

It wasn't until she got home that Zoey got some answers. Her dad told her how sorry he was. He had woken up that morning wanting to watch his daughter play. So he took a double dose of the pain medicine the doctor had given him for his back.

"I had no idea it'd slur my speech and make me obnoxious," he said. "I won't do that again."

"You'd better not," said Zoey. "I've never been so embarrassed."

Exhausted, Zoey crashed on the couch with a glass of chocolate milk and a bowl of peanuts. The TV was on but she wasn't watching. Even though the Sharks were knocked out of the tourney, the weekend had been a success. Kat was still being mean, but Anika and Tia had turned out to be good friends. And Zoey's talk with Mel had worked better than she thought it would. All the girls were passing and they had won their first game. Mel even seemed to be looking for Zoey on the ice now.

Zoey felt part of the team, a true member of the Barrie Sharks. She felt happier than she had in a long time.

★★★

Zoey took that feeling with her into the Sharks' season games. She became more vocal on the ice, calling for passes and urging on teammates. Zoey and Mel began to work more and more together. So did the entire team.

The Sharks started winning. They beat the Mississauga Chiefs 3–2, when Zoey's line combined for two goals and four assists. Against the Markham-Stouffville Stars, Tia broke the 0–0 tie by scoring the winner off a beauty pass from Winnie. Against the Orangeville Tigers, the Sharks mounted a comeback and scored three goals in a great third period of hockey. Zoey set up Mel for the first goal. Tia won the battle for a loose puck and scored the second. Haya banged in a garbage goal to get the win by one.

Zoey found Mel became more and more pleasant — on the ice anyway. She felt her own anger and desire to upstage Mel fade.

Mid-season, the Sharks were in eleventh place of sixteen teams, just three spots out of the playoffs. They were set to face their arch rivals, the Brampton Canadettes. The Sharks and Canadettes had tied their first game, and Zoey was looking forward to the re-match. But she wasn't looking forward to playing against Ting, the beast who'd elbowed her in the head.

"Be careful out there," warned Tia during warm-up.

"Always," said Zoey. "I hope you won't have to jump in to save me again."

The puck dropped and the game was on.

Zoey skated in with Mel and Jan. Jan passed the puck and Zoey snapped a shot wide of the net.

"What kind of dinosaur are you?" said Ting to Zoey as she skated by. "No one uses wooden sticks anymore."

Tia's line kept the puck deep in Brampton's end, but couldn't get a shot.

The Canadettes were all over the Sharks' third line. Anika made save after save.

On her second shift, Mel dangled — fancily deked — a Canadettes defender and saucer passed Zoey a beauty. But Ting poked the puck away from her.

"Nice try, farm girl," said Ting. "But shouldn't you be back in Innisfil dating your cousins?"

Zoey ignored the taunts and skated hard. But in the second period Ting got rougher. The big defender hooked and held and hacked Zoey every time Zoey touched the puck. The Brampton ref wasn't calling any penalties. The Sharks were lucky the period ended without a Canadettes goal.

After the ice surface was flooded and the Zamboni

smoothed out all the skate marks, both teams came out fired up for the third period.

Zoey drew Ting into the corner and fed Mel a pass in the slot. Mel moved the puck quickly to Jan who whacked it into the open side of the net.

Ting responded with a shotgun blast from the blue line, tying the game seconds later. After the goal, she slashed the back of Zoey's leg with her stick. "How do you like that, hotshot?"

"You act like you've never scored before," taunted Zoey. She looked to see if the ref saw the late slash.

"What? Are you going to get your drunken daddy to harass the refs again?" asked Ting.

Zoey was furious. But she held herself back.

Tia had come on the ice before the goal. She had heard everything. "That's pretty low, even for you, Ting," she said.

Ting scowled at the Sharks captain. "Why don't you go back to wherever it is that you came from?"

For Zoey that was the final straw. She tackled Ting and punched her in the ribs again and again. Every time Zoey felt she should stop, she remembered another chirp or slash from Ting. So she punched the defender again.

The ref skated in and with the linesman struggled to pull Zoey off the Brampton defender.

When Ting got up she was holding her side. "I

knew you were trash and this proves it," she spat at Zoey.

The ref threw Zoey out of the game for fighting. Zoey headed off to the dressing room. Ting wasn't penalized for the initial slash or for unsportsmanlike conduct.

The Canadettes controlled the play for the rest of the game. They scored the winning goal on a deflection with three minutes left.

The Sharks had lost to their arch rivals.

After the game, Coach Mikom wasn't pleased. Up to the point when Zoey had been ejected, the team had been playing well. It looked like they could win. "We had the momentum," Coach Mikom said in the change room. "A couple more shifts and we would have put one in."

"We all know whose fault this is. Don't we, Zoey?" said Kat. Mel nodded in agreement.

"Now, now, Kat. We win as a team and we lose as a team," said Coach Mikom.

"Maybe we do. But Zoey has her drunken father's wild temper. She shouldn't be on this team. She's killing us."

"I'll have none of that," said Coach Mikom. Then he turned to Zoey. "Fighting's not like you. What happened out there?"

Zoey hated talking in public, and she hated to complain. But she knew she had to explain. "Ting made a racist comment. I lost my head."

"What did she say?"

"She said, 'Go back to where you came from.'"

"But you were born here, weren't you?" said Coach Mikom. "And your parents, too."

Zoey didn't want to involve Tia if she didn't have to. So she said nothing.

"Coach," Tia broke in. "It was me Ting said that to."

"Oh," said Coach Mikom. "That's a new low, even for Ting."

"That's what I told her," said Tia.

"I'm sorry, Coach," said Zoey. "I shouldn't have beaten on her like that. Like I said, I lost my head. But it won't happen again."

"Next time, tell me and I'll speak with the ref," said Coach Mikom. "And I'll be filing a complaint with my game report."

Though it was hard, Zoey had more to say. "I just want everyone to know that my dad isn't a drunk. He doesn't even drink, really. That game he was slurring his words and yelling at the ref, it was because he took a strong painkiller for his sore back. It was a side effect."

"Thanks for letting us know," said Coach Mikom. "And don't worry. I've heard worse from many parents over the years." He left the room so the girls could undress.

Zoey took off her skates. She was relieved to have explained her dad's condition. Speaking up really did help. Now that she had talked about her concerns, Zoey felt less angry.

Tia rolled the tape from her shin-pads into a ball and threw it at Zoey. "I guess we're even," she said. "Last time we played the Canadettes, I jumped in to defend you. This time you jumped in to defend me."

Zoey gave a small smile. She wasn't proud of what she'd done. She promised herself she'd keep her cool in the future.

11 The ELITE

Zoey was looking forward to the team's second tournament, the North York Elite. It would be the perfect time for her teammates to refocus. They needed to move on from their loss to Brampton and the drama of Ting Chang. Zoey had the money from Lopez's Windows and Doors to cover her hotel and meals. Again, her room would be next to Anika's family's room. Before she left on Friday evening, Zoey confirmed that her father wouldn't show up. She was pretty sure he'd behave if he did, but she was still embarrassed. She wasn't ready for him to come see her play yet.

Minutes after checking in at the hotel, Zoey and Anika rounded up Tia and Marika. They were all up for a game of mini-sticks in Zoey's room. Zoey moved the couch and coffee table into the far corner. Anika dug four Toronto Maple Leafs mini-sticks and a small yellow ball out of her knapsack. Tia set up four plastic cups as goalposts.

"Me and Zoey," said Tia. "I never get to play on her line."

"I guess it's you and me, Marika," said Anika. "We can do this."

The game was as intense as a Stanley Cup final. The four girls took their sports and games seriously. Tia jostled with Anika, who insisted on playing forward. Zoey burned her knees racing for balls. Marika dove into walls to trap wild shots. Anika showed impressive stick-handling skills for a goalie. After thirty minutes of non-stop action, the girls crawled onto Zoey's bed laughing and sweating. No one was officially keeping score, but they all knew Tia and Zoey had won by a goal.

Through text messages, the girls set up a meeting with the rest of the team to check out the hotel. As a group they wandered the halls. They looked into meeting rooms. They sneaked into a wedding reception. They tried out the stationary bikes and equipment in the exercise room. They admired the squash court. And they filled their pockets with caramel candies from the lobby desk. Mel and Kat kept their distance from Zoey and Tia. But all in all the team was one big happy family.

With an hour to curfew, the group disbanded. Anika suggested a quick swim before bed. Anika, Tia and Zoey returned to their rooms to get their bathing suits and then headed down to the pool.

They had the pool to themselves, and the water was

soothing. Zoey floated on her back with her eyes closed. She had friends all around her, a feeling she wasn't quite used to. Tia and Anika were wearing stylish bikinis and Zoey felt self-conscious in her plain blue one-piece. But the thrill of swimming in a heated pool in the middle of winter soon replaced her worries.

The girls slipped from the pool into the bubbling hot tub.

"This is the life," said Anika. "Hockey by day, hot tub by night."

"There's nothing better," said Tia.

"Not even track, Tia?" said Anika. She poked Zoey's arm to get her attention. "Our captain here isn't just a great hockey player. She runs the hundred in 13.4. Tia makes the high school championship each year."

"That's great," said Zoey. "I wish I could sprint."

"My mom was a sprinter growing up," said Tia. "And my dad was a long-distance runner. I'm more shaped like my mom. What other sports do you play?"

"Cricket," said Zoey. "As soon as Anika teaches me."

"In the spring, right after the Sharks win the league championship!" said Anika.

The girls laughed as they dried themselves off. They headed to their rooms in time for curfew.

Saturday morning after breakfast, Zoey and Tia passed the squash court. They looked in through the clear glass wall. A middle-aged couple was ripping balls off every corner of the court and chasing them down.

"That looks fun! I'd like to try it sometime," said Zoey.

"How about now?" said Tia. "After they're done."

"You know how to play?"

"Yeah, my mom taught me. There's a court at our health club."

Zoey was worried. "But I thought we're not supposed to do anything physical before a game. We play in three hours."

"You're right," said Tia. "But I'll just teach you the rules. We won't really play. We'll take it easy."

The girls picked up racquets at the front desk. When they returned to the court it was free.

Tia showed Zoey how to serve. "You start with one foot in your box. You hit the ball off the wall, between the low red line and the top red line. The ball has to land back in your opponent's quarter court." She demonstrated with a high lob that landed right where Zoey was standing. Zoey batted it back off the wall, but it went high out of play. Tia explained the remaining out of bounds lines and gave Zoey some tips. "It's good to try to control the centre of the court. Try to get your opponent running around. And hit hard low shots that bounce right down and are harder to get."

Zoey tried a serve and hit it hard. The ball bounced back into Tia's court. But it was too high off the back wall. When Zoey turned to pick up the ball she saw Kat and Mel scowling at them from the other side of the glass.

Mel opened the door. "You two shouldn't be playing before the game. You know the rules."

"We aren't playing," said Tia. "I'm just teaching Zoey the rules. We're keeping it very low energy."

"Sure," said Kat. "Tell that to the judge."

Mel and Kat shook their heads in disgust and left.

"Do you think we'll get in trouble?" Zoey asked Tia.

"I don't see why," said Tia. "We'd use more energy reading a book."

"They're going to tell Coach Mikom for sure."

"Probably, but he'll understand. Won't he?"

"I don't know about that."

The girls played a few slow rallies. But the fun had gone and they soon packed it in.

★★★

In the lobby before the game, Kat's dad approached Zoey and Tia. "I hope you two have got some energy left for the game."

"What do you mean?" asked Zoey.

"I heard you were playing squash." He turned to Tia. "And you. You're the captain! You should know better."

"We didn't even break a sweat," said Tia.

Zoey hoped that Kat and Mel had reached the end of their need to squeal by telling their parents. But no such luck.

Coach Mikom walked into the change room for the team talk. "Before we begin, there's an issue I have to address."

So much for reaching the end of their need to squeal, thought Zoey.

"It's come to my attention that two team members were playing squash this morning. This is in violation of the team rule against doing strenuous physical activity on game days. Zoey, Tia, is this true?"

"No . . . yes. I was just teaching Zoey the rules," said Tia.

"I'm sorry, but it's a rule," said Coach Mikom. "Squash is an intense sport and we've got three games today."

"But we didn't play intensely. We just practised a few serves," said Tia.

Coach Mikom took a moment to think. He gazed at the two girls and Zoey thought he might be changing his mind. She felt that he wanted to change his mind. But the whole team was watching. And Zoey knew that the coach had to follow his own rules if he expected them to listen to him.

"I'm sorry, girls," he said finally. "But you know the rules. I'll have to bench both of you for the game."

"Bench me, Coach, not Zoey," said Tia. "It was all

my idea. I told her it would be all right."

"No," Coach Mikom said, shaking his head. "You both played squash and you'll both have to sit out the game."

"But we won't make the final if we lose our first game," said Anika.

"You other girls will just have to rise to the occasion," said Coach Mikom. "Next time, Tia, Zoey, put the team first."

Zoey couldn't believe that Coach Mikom would risk the team losing the tournament. Or that Mel would sit silently while her linemate got benched. For the last ten games it was like Mel and Zoey had reached an agreement. They might not have been friends, but they had learned to play well together and win. Zoey hated seeing the steps they had made tossed aside.

12 BENCHED

Zoey and Tia had to sit at the end of the bench, see their teammates struggle and be unable to help. The Sharks were playing the Oakville Hornets. Oakville was a larger town with more skaters to choose from. It was going to be a hard-fought game.

Zoey watched as the Hornets fore-checked aggressively, their forwards skating deep into the Sharks' end and pressuring the defence. They forced turnovers and got pucks to the net. Anika had to make many amazing saves.

Pinned in the Sharks' end, Marika looked exhausted from chasing her opponents.

The Hornets saw early that Mel was the star forward on the Sharks. They covered her closely. Mel rarely got to touch the puck. When she did the Hornets would quickly take away her space and regain possession.

What made it worse was that Zoey knew she and Tia could make a difference out on the ice.

The Hornets' hard work paid off halfway through

the first period. The centre skated in on a Sharks defender and slid the puck between her legs. Then she deked around a tired Anika to score another goal.

The Sharks didn't give up. They came out skating fast in the second period. Nobody wanted to get knocked out of the tournament, so they played hard. But the Hornets kept applying pressure. The Sharks were playing with a short bench and grew more tired each shift. And with Zoey and Tia sitting, the lines were mixed up and the players confused. With two minutes remaining in the period, a Hornets winger scored on a deflection.

The Sharks were two goals down. In this tournament, they had to win all three of their games to get to the final.

During the flood, the girls sat in the change room and tried to catch their breath. Zoey wasn't winded, but she sat with her head down. She was worried that the team was going to lose because she wasn't being played. Early in the game, she had blamed Mel, Kat and Coach Mikom. But as the game went on, Zoey saw that she had no one but herself to blame. She'd been benched because she'd broken a rule. She'd put her own fun above the team's success.

As the coach began to speak, Zoey lifted her head. She wished she could have another chance.

Coach Mikom tried to inspire his players. "You girls are working hard," he said. "Keep it up. We can still turn this around. All we've got to do is —"

"I'm sorry, Coach," said Anika. "But the only way we can turn this around is if you put Zoey and Tia back on the ice. I don't know about you, but I don't want to go home today. I just hope it's not too late."

Zoey watched as furrows formed on Coach Mikom's forehead. He clearly was thinking about Anika's advice.

"Coach, can I say something?" asked Mel.

"Mel, don't make this harder," said Coach Mikom.

"No, no, Coach. I want you to play them," said Mel. "I don't want to go home either."

"I don't know," said Coach Mikom. "There's a clear rule. It has to have firm consequences. I can't overturn all that without good reason."

"I don't think it's fair," said Mel. "The whole team shouldn't have to suffer because two of us broke a rule."

"Why don't we have a vote?" said Anika. "Let the team decide."

"Okay," said Coach Mikom. "All those in favour of Zoey and Tia playing in the third period, please raise your hands."

Hands shot up right away. Everyone's except Kat's, Zoey noticed. Mel nodded at her friend. Kat shrugged and raised her hand, too.

"I see that it's unanimous," said Coach Mikom. "That's good, but not enough. Zoey, Tia, have you learned your lesson?"

"I know I have," said Zoey. "The team always comes first — always. By playing squash I wasted energy that should have been used to help the team."

Tia smiled. "I second that. And I also learned that squash must require much more energy than I ever dreamed. Who knew?"

Coach Mikom laughed. "Awesome, girls! You're back in. Now let's get out there and play like we can. Go Sharks!"

Grateful for a second chance, Zoey stormed onto the ice like she had been denied hockey for years, not for two periods. It felt good to be skating. She loved the cool air in her face, the sound of blades cutting the ice and the feel of her legs crossing as she turned.

The ref dropped the puck. The game was back on. Behind 2–0 against a strong team, the Sharks had their work cut out for them.

Zoey took the puck up ice and dished it to Mel. Mel cut outside. She waited for Jan to arrive in the slot and passed to her. Jan used her opponent as a screen and shot the puck between the defender's legs. The goalie didn't see the shot coming and the Sharks scored.

The Hornets tried to protect their lead. They held back their forwards to keep the Sharks from gaining speed. Zoey saw what they were doing. She dumped the puck into the opposing end and chased it down. She outmuscled the defender for the puck and passed to Mel in the slot. Mel snapped the perfectly placed puck into the top corner of the net.

The game was tied with two-and-a-half minutes left.

Tia split the defence and almost scored the winner.

The Hornets scrambled back up ice and a forward's shot hit the post.

Marika blasted one off the goalie's pads. But no one was there to bury the rebound.

With one minute left, Mel led the charge on left wing with Zoey on her right. Mel passed the puck ahead to Zoey and kept skating past her defender. Zoey gave it back to Mel. Mel picked the top corner to win the game. The goal was just like the Gretzky-Lemieux goal that won Canada the 1987 Canada Cup.

At the buzzer the Sharks smothered Zoey and Mel with hugs.

It was the turning point in the tournament. The momentum carried the Sharks through the next two games. Passing was working, so the girls passed even more. Zoey felt proud to be part of the newfound teamwork. The Sharks beat both Kingston and Sudbury. They would advance to the Sunday final against the London Devilettes.

13 ONE-ON-ONE

Zoey knew that London was a great hockey town. The Devilettes would be a challenge.

She skated onto the ice Sunday morning feeling alive. She'd slept well the night before, buoyed by the Sharks' teamwork and success. Hockey had never been so much fun.

The Devilettes came out skating fast and didn't slow down. After a couple shifts, Zoey got used to their speed. She intercepted a centre-ice pass. She sensed Mel zooming by on her left and sent her a blind pass. Mel crossed the London blue line and rifled a slap shot that the goalie saved.

Near the end of the first period, Mel chased down a loose puck in the corner. She tossed a pass to Zoey who'd just sped into the slot. Zoey fired a wrist shot, but the goalie made a blocker save.

The second period was a battle. London put pressure on the Sharks defence. They forced Anika to jump on a loose puck about to cross the goal-line. Tia hit the post twice. Kat got a roughing penalty for pushing an opponent into the goalpost. With a minute left in the second period, the Devilettes got a breakaway. But Anika didn't fall for the deke.

The Sharks came out fired up for the third period. Zoey and Mel didn't talk much. But they kept up their psychic tie on the ice. With five minutes left, Zoey somehow found Mel by the circle hash marks. Mel's shot rang off the crossbar. With one minute left, Mel passed the puck through Jan's legs and onto Zoey's stick. But Zoey couldn't beat the London goalie.

Regulation time ended with no score.

There would be sudden-death overtime. But not the usual five-on-five, or even four-on-four. There would be two minutes each of four-on-four, three-on-three, two-on-two and one-on-one, until a goal decided the game. Zoey had never heard of anything like it.

Coach Mikom called his players over. They huddled around him. "Zoey, Mel, Marika, Jan — you start. Marika, stay back. Jan, you join the rush when it's safe. Zoey and Mel, work your magic in their end."

"Shouldn't we put Tia and Kat on?" asked Anika. "All our best players?"

"We need to save some for the next shift," said Coach Mikom.

Zoey skated to centre ice. The puck dropped. Zoey drew it back to Marika. Marika passed it up to Mel. Mel took the puck behind the net, left-side. Zoey provided support behind the net, right-side. Mel passed to Zoey. Zoey passed it back. Mel dished it to Jan, who shot low. The goalie made the pad save.

Zoey hustled into the corner to retrieve the rebound. Along the boards, she faked one way and went the other. She sent Mel a pass. Mel rifled a wrist shot off the goalie's shoulder.

The two minute buzzer rang and it was time for a shift change.

The Devilettes attacked with Tia in hot pursuit. They were playing three-on-three and the London forwards had room to skate. Tia and her teammates kept their opponents outside, giving them no chances.

The buzzer rang and Zoey and Mel jumped on ice for the two-on-two. After a rare faceoff loss, Zoey stole the puck back. Mel skated hard into open ice to break free. Zoey fed Mel a stretch pass and Mel dangled the defender. But the goalie made the save. She released the puck to her defender, who skated up ice.

The Sharks changed on the fly to put Tia and Kat on for the last minute of two-on-two. Kat bumped her opponent and stole the puck. She got lucky and no penalty was called. Kat passed to Tia at the blue line. Tia shot the puck quickly to catch the goalie by surprise. The goalie kicked out her leg at the last second and made the save.

The last two-minute buzzer rang. Coach Mikom chose to play Zoey for the first half of one-on-one and

Mel for the second half. He wanted to have fresh legs on for the rest of overtime.

Zoey won the faceoff and skated in on a breakaway. The defender scrambled to catch up but there was no catching Zoey. Zoey shot for the top corner, just missing the mark. The puck bounced off the boards up ice and gave the London skater a twenty-foot advantage. Zoey struggled to catch up, thrusting her legs. It looked hopeless. But by the time she reached the far blue line Zoey had lifted her opponent's stick and stolen the puck.

As she carried the puck past the bench, Zoey was tired. She knew she was supposed to change. There was only one minute left and it was Mel's turn to play. But Zoey was on a breakaway. This was as good a chance to score as the Sharks could hope for. So Zoey didn't dump the puck. This was her chance to win it all.

Coach Mikom yelled as she skated by. "Change it up, Zoey! Change! Change!"

Kat was furious. "Get off the ice, girl," she called. "Now!"

Zoey didn't listen. The lane to the net was clear. She thought it would be crazy to give away the puck. This time she'd dangle. She came in close. She faked a shot. She deked right, she deked left. She put the puck between the goalie's legs in an unbelievable triple-deke.

The Sharks had won the tournament!

Anika tackled Zoey. Zoey felt all her teammates, including Mel, jump on the pile. Not all of her teammates.

Kat hovered by, sulking. The weight of the team on Zoey's body wasn't comfortable. And it was smelly. But Zoey could have stayed buried forever.

Coach Mikom wasn't happy. "Zoey, you should have come off when I told you," he said. "We had a plan, and you changed it. You're just lucky we didn't pay the price."

Zoey was shocked. "We didn't," she said.

"But we could have. And next time we will. I thought you learned that no one player is more important than the team. Now do you understand?"

"It's just that I was on a breakaway. I made a judgment call."

"Well, it was the wrong call. The Sharks needed fresh legs out there. And Mel deserved her chance to make something happen."

Zoey thought about how tired she'd been when her shift should have ended. She'd already made one rush and a gruelling back-check when she headed up ice for her second rush. Things could easily have ended badly. If Zoey hadn't scored, the fresh Devilette would have picked up the puck. Zoey would have been too tired to catch her. Zoey thought about how sad and angry she would be if Mel played through her turn on the ice. Coach Mikom was right.

"I'm sorry, Coach," she said softly. "I'll come off next time."

"That's better," said Coach Mikom. "It's a learning

process, Zoey. And you've come a long way. Next time you'll make the right decision."

"I'll do my best," said Zoey. "I love this team."

"I know you will. And nice goal, by the way."

14 MUST WIN

The Sharks' tournament win carried over into the regular season. The team won five games straight. They moved from eleventh place to ninth, one point behind the Leaside Wildcats. Zoey felt her on-ice connection with Mel grow stronger every game. But she didn't like that Kat still resented her presence. There seemed to be nothing she could do to win Kat over. The exciting — and scary — thing was that the Sharks' last game was against the Wildcats. A victory would earn the Sharks the last playoff spot.

Riding with Anika through Leaside to the arena, Zoey was impressed by the pretty tree-lined streets and brick houses. As they walked through the arena's lobby, she admired the long down parkas and high leather boots of the Leaside mothers. *Hockey is great*, she thought. Before joining the Sharks she'd never heard of Leaside. Now she was seeing wonderful new places and people.

In the change room, Mel turned to Zoey. It was the

first time Mel spoke to Zoey off-ice since her insults when Zoey first made the team. "These Leaside parents are such snobs, don't you think? Walking around in fancy jackets. So high and mighty."

Zoey was surprised. "I don't know anything about that, Mel. But I hope we give their kids a good beating." Zoey found it funny that the biggest snob on the Sharks team was the one who thought the Leaside parents were snobs.

On the ice, Zoey set up for the opening faceoff. The ref had a long face and an upturned nose. He looked Zoey up and down and waved her out of the circle. Zoey checked her feet. One was slightly over the line. No one had ever waved her out for that.

Mel came to take the faceoff. As she skated by Zoey, she whispered, "I told you they were snobs. This ref's a homer, for sure."

"What do you mean?" asked Zoey.

"He's gonna favour the home team."

Zoey played even more intensely than usual. She took the puck wide, skating around the Wildcats' net and back towards the blue line. She dished Mel a backhand pass as if she could see through the back of her head. Mel faked a shot. The goalie went down and Mel shot over the fallen body.

The Sharks were up 1–0. Zoey controlled the pace whenever she was on the ice. Halfway through the first period, she stickhandled through three opponents. She slipped a backhand under the goalie.

The Sharks had a two-goal lead.

The Wildcats started hooking and slashing Zoey. Several times Zoey looked to the ref, expecting a penalty to be called. None was.

Near the end of the second period, Zoey intercepted a pass. She skated in on a breakaway. The Wildcats defender dove and swept her stick along the ice, bringing Zoey down. Since the defender's stick made no contact with the puck, a tripping penalty should have been called. Or even a penalty shot, as Zoey was on a breakaway. But the ref stayed silent.

Zoey got up and skated to the ref. "How was that not tripping?" she asked.

"Play on," said the ref. "And don't be such a whiner."

Zoey couldn't believe it. Was the ref insulting her? Mel's claim that the Leaside parents were snobs might or might not be true. But Zoey was beginning to believe that the ref favoured the Wildcats. It wasn't like they hadn't ever had a ref be a bit biased. But this was a big game. It was unfair.

The Wildcats came out hard in the third period. They saw they could get away with anything. So they amped up their hooking, holding and cross-checking. Zoey couldn't skate two feet without being whacked and jabbed. This wore down the Sharks. They couldn't keep their momentum.

When Zoey was pinned against the boards by a winger, the Wildcats centre saw her chance. She picked a goal into the top corner of Anika's net. A minute later, she sped around the net and scored a wraparound goal. Zoey couldn't stop her because the Leaside winger was holding Zoey's jersey in front of the net.

Scowling at the ref, Zoey grabbed the front of her own shirt and pulled to show holding. "Didn't you see that? The girl held me so tight my jersey's three sizes bigger!"

"Don't be such a drama queen," said the ref.

Zoey skated to the bench, shaking her head. The game was tied.

With Zoey's line silenced, Tia fought hard to mount a comeback. But the Wildcats manhandled her, too. With the Sharks one point behind the Wildcats in the standings, they needed a win to make the playoffs. A tie just wouldn't do.

Zoey looked at the clock. There were only four minutes left in regulation time. The Sharks had the puck in the Wildcats' end. But they couldn't get a clear shot.

Zoey had to break free from the stifling coverage. She skated towards the bench as if she were changing. But she stopped and waited along the boards. She lay low for a moment, then skated back to the side of the net. Mel saw her in the clear and sent a pass. It looked like a sure goal. All Zoey had to do was tap the puck into the open corner. But as the puck was about to hit Zoey's stick, a Wildcats defender raced in and slew-footed her down. The puck slid off into the corner.

Zoey was livid. Seeing the ref hadn't called a penalty, she jumped up. She cross-checked the guilty defender, who fell to the ice.

Right away, the whistle blew. The ref skated to the time-keeper's box. "Barrie number 10, two minutes, cross-checking," he announced. He was giving Zoey a penalty.

Zoey challenged the ref. "Why wasn't there a call on the slew-foot?"

"Stop that or I'll give you another two minutes."

"You must have seen it!" said Zoey. "You were right there."

"Look, back in Barrie you might get away with all the cross-checks you want. But around here we play by the rules."

"Yeah, right," said Tia. "What about rules about slew-footing? Why didn't you make the initial call?" As captain, she deserved an explanation. But she didn't get one.

"This is your last chance," the ref told Zoey. "Get to the box."

Zoey did what he said and skated towards the penalty box. But Tia was furious. "No," she said to the ref. "This is your last chance to be fair, not a lying, cheating homer!"

"Number 9, you're out!" said the ref, pointing at Tia.

"What for?" asked Tia.

"Unsportsmanlike conduct and abusing a referee."

Tia skated towards the penalty box.

"Not there, right out. You're out of this game," said the ref. "And the next."

"You can't do that!" said Tia.

"I just did," said the ref. "Get off the ice or I'll give you another game."

Tia skated off.

Coach Mikom tried to complain, but the ref wouldn't listen. He told his players he'd be filing a formal complaint.

Zoey's two-minute penalty started with two-twenty left in the game. She couldn't believe the unfairness of the ref. He seemed to look down on the Barrie players the same way Mel and Kat looked down on Zoey and Innisfil.

On the power play, the Wildcats forwards were all over the Sharks. They didn't need to score. All they needed was a tie to advance to the playoffs.

The Sharks appeared doomed with twenty seconds left.

But then Zoey's penalty was done. She jumped out of the box.

She crossed the red line. She was behind Leaside's last defender.

Crossing the Sharks' blue line, Mel saw Zoey in the clear. She sent Zoey a crisp stretch pass.

Zoey reined in the pass and took the puck across the Wildcats' blue line.

The Wildcats defender was hot on Zoey's tail. She reached with her stick to poke the puck. But Zoey stretched her leg to protect the puck. She rifled a wrist shot into the top corner of the net.

Zoey had scored the winning goal in the last seconds of the game.

The Barrie Sharks had beaten the Leaside Wildcats to claim eighth place in the league. They had a spot in the playoffs for the first time in ten years.

Kat praised Mel's pass. But she said nothing to Zoey. The other Sharks all gave her hugs. Zoey couldn't understand why Kat wouldn't be happy, too.

15 PROMOTED

Two days before the quarter-final, Coach Mikom had the Sharks working hard in practice. Power play, penalty kill, breakout, deflections off shots from the point.

As the team left the ice, the coach told Zoey he wanted to talk to her. He had her sit beside him on the bench.

Coach Mikom smiled. "With Tia out, I have to find someone to captain the quarter-final game."

"Who are you thinking of? Mel? Kat?"

"They're both great players. But I want to talk to you."

Zoey shifted nervously on the bench. "I don't know, Coach. Mel and Kat are already assistants. I can't score like Mel, and Kat is solid on defence. And they've both been on the team for years."

"Zoey, your playmaking skills and work ethic have turned this team around. But if I'm going to make you captain, I have to be sure you're prepared to be a team player. You've got to come off when I tell you to come off. And you can't lose your cool like you did in the tournament. A captain has to be selfless and lead by example. Do you think you can do that?"

Zoey was scared. "I don't think I deserve it, Coach. I'm so competitive and sometimes selfish out there. I'm trying, but —"

"I can see you're trying, Zoey." The coach smiled. "No one works harder. And you never give up. I've watched your attitude improve the past few months. I know you got everyone passing. And you encourage your teammates. Think of this as a chance to prove yourself."

"But why take a chance on me?"

Coach Mikom leaned back on the bench to stretch. "When I started playing, I was a really competitive young player. No one hogged the puck more than I did. But my coach saw something that even I didn't know was there. He taught me to put the team first. I learned that it didn't matter who scored as long as the team was successful. Eventually he made me captain. And I became this model of sportsmanship and team-play you know and love."

Zoey laughed. "Okay, Coach, I'll do it."

"Awesome," said Coach Mikom. "You'll do a great job. And don't forget, it's only temporary. Tia will be back."

★★★

"I hear you've been made captain," said Anika to Zoey. They were headed to North Simcoe to play the

Capitals. "You must be so happy!"

"I know you'll do a great job," said Anika's dad, glancing at Zoey in his rearview mirror.

Zoey was worried that some of her teammates wouldn't be as happy about it as Anika. *All I can do*, she thought, *is try my best to control my temper. And put the Sharks first at all times.*

The North Simcoe Capitals had finished the regular season in first place. The game would be a challenge for the Sharks. Zoey hoped she could handle the extra pressure.

In the change room, Coach Mikom announced that he'd made Zoey captain. The team cheered, except for Mel who ignored the news and Kat who glared at Zoey. Carla taped a 'C' onto Zoey's jersey and patted her back. Zoey was proud of the progress she had made with Mel on and off the ice. She hoped this wouldn't set them back and ruin the connection they had now.

"Play like we can," said Coach Mikom as the girls stormed out onto the ice. "Goooooo, Shaaarrrksss!"

The ref dropped the puck. The game was on.

The Capitals won the faceoff. The Simcoe skaters seemed even faster than they had been earlier in the season. Zoey felt like a dog chasing her own tail as she struggled to catch the forwards in her end.

The Sharks' second line fared no better. The Simcoe defence pinched along the boards and the Sharks couldn't break out.

The Sharks' third line battled hard. Alice pressed her opponent against the boards. Trisha passed the loose puck forward to Haya, and Haya dumped it into the Simcoe end. The three forwards raced across the blue line. Haya beat the defender to the puck and passed to Alice, who one-timed a slap shot off the post.

On her second shift, Zoey wanted to make a difference. She won the faceoff and drew the puck back to Marika. Marika skated ahead and passed back to Zoey. Zoey passed to Mel. But the Simcoe centre intercepted the pass. She skated in and scored.

It was 1–0. It stayed that way through the second period.

Every time Zoey thought Mel was open and passed it to her, a Capitals player would race in and scoop up the puck. Every time Jan powered down the wing, a Capitals player would catch up, lift her stick and steal it. Zoey had never played a team that skated so fast and covered so much ice. But she noticed that Haya, Alice and Trisha — the third-line grinders — kept getting chances.

The Sharks returned to the ice for the third period fired up. Coach Mikom had given an inspiring speech that fired up the girls who knew their season was on the line. But the Capitals kept controlling the play. With each passing minute, the morale of the team was going down.

With two minutes left, Coach Mikom called a time-out. The Sharks gathered round. "As soon as we get the chance, we'll pull the goalie," he said. "Right now, I want our five best out. Zoey, Mel, Winnie, Kat and Marika. Jan, as soon as Anika comes off, you hop on as the extra attacker. Now, go get 'em, girls!"

The huddle was about to break when Zoey piped up. "Coach, I think we should play Haya's line."

There was silence. Kat turned to Zoey in shock.

"I don't know about that," said Sue.

"No, really," said Zoey. "They've been getting the best chances all game."

Coach Mikom thought for a moment. "What does everyone think?" he asked.

"I think Zoey's right," said Mel. "Play the grinders. And Jan when Anika comes off."

"I agree," said Anika.

Zoey's head snapped up when Kat spoke. "I do too," she said.

So Haya, Alice and Trisha took the ice, along with Kat and Marika.

The puck dropped. Alice dug it out of the corner and dumped it into the Simcoe end. Anika came out of the net and Jan took her place on the ice. Haya chased the puck down and passed it out to Trisha. As Trisha was falling, she whacked the spiralling rubber over the goalie's leg.

It wasn't pretty but it was a goal. The game was tied with one minute left.

Haya and her linemates came off the ice.

Before the faceoff, Mel skated to Zoey. "Zoey,

they know you're a playmaker," Mel said. "They've been intercepting our passes all game. How about you hog the puck for a change?"

"Are you sure?" asked Zoey.

"I have enough goals this year," said Mel. "Let's see your dangles."

Zoey won the faceoff and tapped the puck forward. She picked up her own draw and skated in.

The Capitals wingers covered Mel and Jan, waiting for Zoey to pass.

The Capitals centre chased Zoey down. Zoey waited for her opponent to reach for the puck. She dragged it towards her left foot, and then over to her right foot. Then she sped up.

Zoey passed the centre. She dragged the puck behind her own body and pushed it into her skate. Then she kicked it forward and shot by the defender — a between-the-legs toe drag. What seemed a hopeless rush was now a breakaway.

Zoey dangled twice. Then she snapped a rocket over the goalie's blocker as the buzzer rang.

The Sharks had won the quarter-final.

Mel was first to jump on Zoey. Everyone except Kat followed. When Zoey broke free from the team embrace, she turned to Haya, Alice and Trisha to rave about their game-saving goal. As Zoey skated off the ice, she caught Kat nodding. It wasn't a friendly nod, but it was something.

16 SHAKEN

Once she had finished her chores Saturday morning, Zoey didn't know what to do with herself. The semi-final wasn't till four p.m. She was restless. It was exciting to be playing the Sharks' arch rivals, the Brampton Canadettes. And Zoey was eager to hand being captain back to her friend. She had enjoyed leading the team, but the role was rightly Tia's. What Zoey wasn't looking forward to was playing against Ting Chang.

Zoey put on her boots but no coat. She grabbed a road-hockey stick and went out on the porch. She practised her stick-handling with a puck placed on a plastic sheet. She took shots into an old beat-up net. Her father had placed a large rectangular board behind the goal to stop wild shots from flying across the yard. He had also hung detergent jugs in the four corners of the net as targets. After thirty minutes of aiming at the jugs, Zoey pulled out a soccer ball and juggled it. She kept it in the air with her feet, knees, chest and head for 170 touches, a new record. When she was done she went inside. She watched the movie *The Mighty Ducks* while eating the tuna casserole her mother had made for lunch.

As the movie ended, her father entered the family room.

"Good luck in your game, Zoey," he said. "I'm sorry I can't make it. But my back's been feeling much better. If you can win one more, I think I'll be fine to come to the final. Can you win one more for me?"

"I'll do my best, Dad," she said. "But the Canadettes are tough as nails."

"That may be," he said. "But they can't be half as tough as this small-town Innisfil farm girl."

"Dad, that's embarrassing," Zoey said. But she found herself smiling.

★★★

During the warm-up, Zoey couldn't rein in a wild pass. She skated over the red line into the Brampton end to retrieve the puck. She was stick-handling back when she felt a stick blade hit her calf from behind. The hit was so hard it hurt.

Zoey stumbled and turned. "What the heck?"

Ting was in her face. "You'd better keep your head up, Hayseed. Because there's a big red target on your back today."

"Do I look worried?" asked Zoey.

"As a matter of fact, you do," said Ting. "Don't think I've forgotten those punches to the ribs. Or the suspension I got for chirping your captain."

"It's one thing to chirp. It's another to make racist insults."

"I didn't mean it like that," said Ting.

"Well, next time, think about what you're saying," said Zoey.

Ting shrugged and skated away. Zoey headed back to her bench for Coach Mikom's pep talk.

He reminded his team that the Canadettes were a good defensive team. He told them to use the offence strategies they'd worked on in practice. He also stressed the need to avoid the penalty box. "If we're disciplined," he said, "we can beat this team."

Zoey's worries left the moment the puck was dropped.

Following the coach's advice about offence, Zoey kept her stick on the ice to give her teammates a target. She skated hard to give her linemates close support. The Sharks passed well, but they couldn't get through the Canadettes' defence.

Midway through the first period, Brampton controlled the play in the Sharks' end. The Brampton forwards circled along the boards, passing the puck back and forth, until Ting stepped in from the point. The winger passed to her. Zoey had the centre covered. But all she could do was watch as Ting wound up and one-timed a blaster. It went through the crowded slot and over Anika's shoulder.

The Canadettes were up 1–0.

Tia skated through the neutral zone with speed. But Ting maintained a perfect gap between them and poke-checked the puck away.

Zoey followed Tia's lead, speeding through the neutral zone. She dished the puck to Mel and drove through the middle to the net. This pulled the defenders back to protect their goal area, and gave Mel space to skate in. She sniped a wrist shot.

Thanks to Zoey's smart play, the game was tied.

Five minutes into the second period, Ting banged a pass off the boards. Zoey was about to retrieve the loose puck when Ting rushed in and held Zoey's jersey. But the ref didn't see and no penalty was called. The Brampton centre snatched the puck, beat the last defender and scored on a backhand to the top of the net.

The Canadettes again had the lead.

Ten seconds later, on a two-on-one, Alice slipped the puck under a diving defender. Haya shot into the open side of the net. The Sharks' third line had tied the game.

The rest of the period was scoreless.

During the flood, Coach Mikom praised his team. "Girls, you're playing well. Keep up the great teamwork and aggressive offence. We can do this. Goooo, Sharks!"

Zoey came out for the third period eager to put this game to bed. She crossed the blue line and dropped a pass to Jan. Jan hit Mel with a short pass. Zoey raced towards the net. Mel fed Zoey what should have been a sure goal. But at the last moment Ting charged and crushed Zoey head on in an illegal check. Zoey's stomach bore the worst of the hit. She fell backwards, writhing in pain.

Tia was half over the boards to revenge the hit. But Coach Mikom pulled her back. "We can't afford the penalty," he said.

"But they didn't give Ting a penalty," said Tia.

"That's the point," said Coach Mikom. "We can't afford to lose you."

Zoey lay on her back on the ice struggling to breathe. Mel — who'd never fought in her life — threw off her pink gloves and started swinging at Ting.

"Mel, we can't afford to lose you either!" shouted Coach Mikom.

Jan tried to pull Mel back. But there was no stopping her.

Wild fists were flying until the ref and linesman could each grab one of the girls and hold her. Both Ting and Mel received major penalties for fighting and were ejected from the game.

Carla knelt on the ice by Zoey, who was still struggling to breathe. After confirming that the injury wasn't a concussion, Carla had Zoey sit in a crouched position. "I think you're winded," said Carla. "Sitting up will relax your diaphragm. I know it's hard, but try to be calm. Take slow, deep breaths."

Both teams gathered by their respective benches and the arena was silent. Zoey sat breathing in and out slowly.

After four or five minutes, Zoey was breathing a little better. Carla helped her to her feet. Zoey held Tia's arm with one hand and Marika's with the other. The two Sharks helped their shaken teammate off the ice.

17 Return TO PLAY

Carla went with Zoey to the change room. She told Zoey to sit in a crouched position and to keep breathing in and out.

After five minutes, Zoey stood up and said, "My breathing's fine. Can I play now?"

"How's your head?" asked Carla. "Do you have a headache or feel any pressure there?"

"You told me I was winded," said Zoey. "Not that I have a concussion."

"Yes, but you could have hit your head when you fell. We have to be safe."

"I promise I didn't hit my head. I wouldn't lie about that. My stomach and back are a little sore. But I'm fine."

"Well, let's head back to the bench. You can rest there for five. Then we'll see if you're good to go for the last five minutes."

The two returned to the Sharks' bench. There were nine minutes left in the third period and the score was still tied.

Coach Mikom smiled and patted Zoey's shoulder. He consulted with Carla, then said, "Take it easy for a while, Zoey. You don't want to go back on before you're ready."

Zoey sat at the end of the bench. She watched the Canadettes hold the Sharks in their own end and pound Anika with pucks. Zoey couldn't watch her team struggle without wanting to help. She was itching to jump over the boards and get to work. Anika was making amazing saves and keeping the Sharks in the game. But how much longer could they expect Anika to stand on her head between the pipes? And how much longer before the Canadettes took the lead and sent the Sharks packing?

With Zoey and Mel out, Coach Mikom double-shifted Tia. At full strength, Tia could power-skate the puck out of the Sharks' end any time she wanted. But as fit Tia was, the extra ice time was wearing her down. She was moving more slowly. The Canadettes were easily chasing her down and stealing the puck.

Not being able to play was unbearable to Zoey. "Put me in, Coach," she said. "I'm fine. I really am."

Coach Mikom looked at the time clock. "Not just yet," he said.

The Canadettes continued to control the play. With five minutes left, one of their forwards broke free on a breakaway. Her shot hit the post. Zoey was frantic. She saw her season ending. She saw her father not getting to see one last game, the final. Zoey pleaded with Coach Mikom, "Please, please, please, put me on. It's my fault that Mel got thrown out. I want to make up for it."

Coach Mikom turned to Carla for guidance.

Carla looked at Zoey standing in front of the bench, raring to go.

And then Kat said, "Just put her on. She's tough. And she wants to help the team."

Zoey couldn't believe her ears. Kat, of all people, wanted her to play. And she thought Zoey was tough.

"Yes, put her on," said Carla. "She's had the extra five minutes of rest I wanted."

With four minutes left in the game, Zoey jumped the boards.

Her first shift back on, Zoey worked with Tia to move the puck into the Canadettes' end. They applied pressure, but couldn't score.

Inspired by Zoey's return, Haya's line stepped up their play. Alice tipped a deflection just wide of the net.

Zoey hopped back on with one minute left. She scooped up a loose puck and crossed the red line. Nearing a Brampton defender, she flipped the puck up high into the air over the defender's head. It fell behind the defender. Zoey skated to the puck and in on the goalie. She faked left, then pulled right. She fired a backhand over the goalie's shoulder into the top corner of the net.

The Sharks had a one-goal lead with twenty-two seconds left.

The ref dropped the puck at centre ice. Zoey drew it back to Marika. Marika skated across the red line and dumped it into the Canadettes' end. Tia fore-checked hard and tied up the defender with the puck in the corner.

The buzzer sounded. The Sharks had won the semi-final!

The team swarmed Zoey. Once more, everyone piled on but Kat.

When Zoey broke free from the pile, she saw Ting on one side of the stands. The big defender looked crushed. Zoey saw Mel smiling and waving from the other end of the stands. The two brawlers couldn't come onto the ice. Zoey felt sad because she wanted to thank Mel.

As the Sharks skated off, Kat said, "Nice goal, Hayseed. You farm girls have some game."

Zoey wasn't fond of the nickname. But this time it was said with surprising affection. She realized she didn't have to take it as an insult. *Kat is tough and a team player*, thought Zoey. *She must respect that I returned to play and tried to make up for losing Mel.*

Zoey joined her teammates in the dressing room. She smiled happily at Mel sitting in her street clothes. "Nice upper-cuts!" Zoey said. "I think we've found our new enforcer."

"It was kind of a rush," said Mel. "I've wanted to punch Ting for a long time. But I think I'll stick to scoring the goals. I wouldn't want to put Tia out of work."

"Hey, I'm willing to share," said Tia.

Everyone on the team laughed.

***

Anika's dad drove Zoey home. "I've never seen anyone do that flip move before," he said. "I didn't think it was possible."

"It was my first time doing it," said Zoey. "I got lucky, I guess,"

"That wasn't luck," said Anika. "That was skill."

"It certainly was," said Anika's dad.

"Are you going to the CWHL game tomorrow?" Zoey asked Anika.

"Of course. The whole team is," said Anika. "Aren't you?"

"Yeah, for sure!" said Zoey. "Who's playing?"

"The Toronto Furies and Les Canadiennes."

"That should be a good one."

Getting out of the van, Zoey found her dad waiting on the front porch. "Well?" he said. "How did it go?"

"We won, Daddio! We're off to the final!"

"That's awesome. Did you have a good game?"

"Well, I got knocked on my butt and winded. But

I came back to score the winning goal."

"Way to go, Zoey! Please tell me you're okay."

"Yeah, I'm fine. Will you be able to come with Mom to the final?"

"Yes, for sure. I'm feeling much better and wouldn't miss it. I should be able to get back to working the farm this Monday."

Zoey was thrilled that her father would be coming to her game. But part of her was a little worried. "Don't take too much of that pain medication," she said.

"Certainly not," he said laughing. "I learned my lesson. That poor ref! In fact, I don't think I'll have to take any meds. The pain's gone and the doctor has given me a clean bill of health."

At the beginning of the season, Zoey had been embarrassed for her dad — the farmer — to even set foot in the arena. But the more she saw of other adults, the more she appreciated his honesty and support. *When he makes a mistake, like taking too many painkillers and acting obnoxious, he apologizes*, she thought. *Not like some hockey parents who scream at their kids. Or refs who make bad calls.*

18 NIGHT OUT

That Wednesday, the Sharks met at the Barrie Allandale Recreation Centre for the bus that would take them to the Mastercard Centre. There they would watch the Toronto Furies play Les Canadiennes de Montréal. It was Zoey's first time attending a pro women's hockey game and she was excited. The bus ride was only forty minutes long, but Zoey was looking forward to them all having fun on the way.

Zoey took a seat in the fifth row beside Anika. They were behind Tia and Marika. Anika paused her music and took out her earphones.

"Blasting some tunes?" asked Zoey.

"Oh yeah, getting pumped," said Anika.

Zoey smiled. "I'm really looking forward to this game. Most of my favourite players will be playing."

"I know, I'm excited, too," said Anika. "And so many of them have won Olympic gold medals and world championships."

"Yeah, that's awesome!" said Zoey. "I wish I could

play like that."

For most of the trip the four girls played euchre. Tia and Marika kneeled backwards on their seats. Tia partnered with Zoey and Marika with Anika. The girls laughed when Marika kept forgetting what suit had to be played. And Anika threw her hands in the air in mock outrage the second time Zoey hinted illegally at what cards Tia should play.

The bus parked in the Mastercard Centre lot. The team headed into the lobby of the best hockey facility in Greater Toronto. The Canadian Women's Hockey League game was to be played on Rink 3 in one hour. Coach Mikom called the girls over to Rink 4. He was standing by the window with other fans looking in on the ice. "Girls, I think you might want to watch this."

Zoey and Anika squeezed through the crowd and took a look.

"I can't believe it!" said Zoey. "It's the Maple Leafs!"

"That's right, Zoey," said Coach Mikom. "I got us here a little early to watch the Leafs practise."

The other Sharks elbowed their way to the window.

"Incredible," said Tia.

"So cool," said Mel.

"Look! They're doing the same break-out drill we do," said Zoey.

"But much smoother," said Tia.

"I can't believe I'm seeing all of my favourite stars in person," said Mel.

"I just love the top line," said Zoey. "Bing-bing-bing and it's in."

"I wish I could skate backwards as fast as the defence," said Marika.

After the break-outs, the Leafs worked a high tempo passing drill. Every pass was hard. Every pass was tape to tape. The Leafs skaters made it look easy.

Next came a shooting drill. Anika watched with a look of wonder as the goalie shut down the Leafs forwards. "He's always in the right position," she said. "And he moves from side to side so well."

As the practice was winding down, a public relations officer for the Maple Leafs came out. She gave each of the girls a big loot bag filled with Maple Leafs pucks, mini-sticks and balls, water-bottles, toques and skate-wiping towels.

"It's like Christmas," said Tia.

"No, it's even better," said Zoey.

Coach Mikom led the girls to Rink 3. They took their centre-ice seats, just five rows up in the stands. Zoey sat between Mel and Anika. Tia and Marika were in front one row down. Haya and Alice sat two rows down. The rest of the Sharks were scattered in groups nearby. Coach Mikom sat with Carla one row behind Zoey. All the girls were laughing and joking as the game began.

The Furies won the opening faceoff and the centre controlled the puck. Zoey thought the Furies captain was even faster than she looked on TV during her games with Team Canada. Zoey and Tia were die-hard Toronto fans, but Mel and Anika were cheering on Les Canadiennes.

When the Furies scored halfway through the first period, Tia howled in pleasure. Anika bombarded her with a handful of peanuts. Tia jumped up and chased Anika to the top of the stands and around the rink.

At the first intermission, everyone went to get drinks and nachos except Zoey and Mel. The two girls stayed in their seats. Zoey wondered if Mel would talk to her. She resolved she would wait for Mel to be the first to say something.

"So what's it like living on a farm in a small town?" asked Mel. "I don't think I could do it. I know Barrie's not that big. But it's a lot bigger than Innisfil."

Zoey thought for a moment. "Actually, it's not that bad," she said. "In fact, I love it. The air is so fresh — most of the time, anyway." She laughed. "And the sky at night is big and clear and filled with stars. All our neighbours are friendly. Everyone says hi in the grocery store and on the main street. And when something bad happens, or anything needs to be done, everyone pulls together. Oh, and I love animals — except lambs."

"What do you have against lambs?" asked Mel.

"When I was a toddler, I was afraid that one would break into our house."

"And do what? Cuddle you to death?"

"Yeah, exactly. See, you get it. And they've got those hoof things. I just hate them."

Mel laughed. "Well, it's great that you love life out there in the boonies. Me, I think I'll stay a city girl."

Everyone was back in their seats to see Les Canadiennes score the tying goal one minute into the second period. This time Anika cheered loudly and Tia pelted her with a handful of popcorn.

Zoey and Mel visited the washroom together between the second and third periods. On the way back, they stopped at the concession stand. Mel bought fries that she shared with Zoey at a small table.

"I'd love to go pro one day," said Mel. "At least that's what I'm hoping for. How about you?"

"I'd like to," said Zoey. "But I'm not good enough. And even if I was, I couldn't afford to play. I'm gonna have to work to pay the bills."

"Don't sell yourself short," said Mel. "You're as good as — in fact, better than — anyone I've played with. And look at this season. You made it work out with all the funding you raised. Don't forget, the CWHL players get paid now. It's not much, not like the millions NHL players make. But it's a start."

"I didn't know that about the CWHL," said Zoey. "All I know is that I love to play more than anything.

We'll see what happens. I'm not stopping anytime soon."

"That's good news for the Sharks," said Mel. She smiled. "I'm glad you came out this year." She paused. "And . . . I'm sorry I was such a —"

"Don't worry about it," said Zoey. "We worked it all out, didn't we?"

"We sure did. We're up for the league championship!"

The third period was an action-packed battle that ended a tie. So neither Tia nor Anika earned bragging rights.

Coach Mikom walked with Zoey to the bus. "That was a great game," he said.

"It was," she said. "Thanks for taking us. And for the Leafs practice."

"My pleasure," said Coach Mikom.

"I love how the women play," said Zoey. "There's so much skating and passing. And not as many delays for fighting . . . I've been thinking since I got thrown out of that game for pounding on Ting — there's just no need to fight. Hockey is rough and tough enough without it."

As Zoey got on the bus she thought how great it would be to play at the professional level.

19 The FINAL

The day of the big game had arrived. The Sharks were playing the Aurora Panthers for the league championship. The Panthers had finished the season in second place. They had won both their regular season games against the Sharks. And they had knocked the Sharks out of the Burlington Splash tournament. But what worried Zoey most had nothing to do with hockey play. It had been the Panthers parents who had seen her father's abuse of the referee. And her father would be attending this final game. *If someone gives him a hard time*, thought Zoey, *I'll want to die.*

In the change room, Coach Mikom gave his pre-game talk. "Play like you've played all season," he said. "And leave everything on the ice. Oh, and make sure you watch number 4 and number 18 closely. You know who they are. I hear both have already been scouted by the Canadian National Women's Under-18 team."

During warm-up, Zoey glanced at her parents in the stands. They'd changed out of their work clothes and looked nice. But she couldn't help thinking that the Aurora parents were giving her dad the stink eye.

The puck dropped and the Panthers took control. Their captain, number 4, wasn't that big for a defender. But her bulky shoulder pads and extra-long stick, combined with aggressive play, made her a looming presence.

The Sharks didn't get to touch the puck for the first five minutes. But they were playing well defensively. They didn't give the Panthers any good scoring chances — until number 4 blasted a slap shot from the blue line off of Anika's pads. The puck popped out and dropped. Before it even hit the ice, number 18 knocked the puck up and over, keeping it in the air. Then she batted it into the open side of the net. It was an amazing display of hand-eye coordination. The Panthers were up 1–0.

Zoey tried to mount several rushes. But the Panthers took away her time and space and regained possession.

Tia fore-checked hard. But the Panthers were always one step ahead.

Haya dumped the puck into the Panthers' end, but the Panthers won the race to the puck and skated back up ice.

Kat was playing the game of her life. She angled the Panthers forwards into the corner and stole the puck, again and again. But just as quickly the Panthers would get it back.

The Final

With twenty-seconds left in the first period, Zoey came on for a faceoff in the Sharks' zone. The puck dropped, and before Zoey could react, number 18 had snapped it into the top corner of the Sharks' net. A goal right off the draw! The Sharks were down by two.

Between periods, Coach Mikom told the Sharks that they were playing well. He said that the Panthers were a high-scoring team. Keeping them to two goals was an achievement. "Keep it up," he said. "But we have to shut down number 18. Tia, for the rest of the game, we'll play your line against hers. I want you to stick to her like glue. If she goes for a drink of water, I want you there holding the bottle. Understand?"

"Sure thing, Coach. I'm on her," said Tia.

"Good. Zoey, this will also free your line up," said Coach Mikom. "You should end up with a lot more time and space playing against their second line."

As the period began, Zoey looked to the stands where her parents were sitting quietly. No one was bothering them. No one was paying them any attention. Her mother waved and tried to get her husband to wave. But he sat up straight with his hands on his lap and his eyes glued to the ice. Seeing this calmed Zoey's nerves and let her focus on her play.

Tia shadowed number 18, staying between her and the puck. The Sharks captain broke up several passes and tied number 18 up behind the net. The Panthers star forward couldn't get a shot or a scoring chance.

Number 18 slashed Tia and got a penalty. The Sharks couldn't score during the power play. But slowly they started to break down the Panthers' rhythm.

Halfway through, Zoey was pinned face to the boards in the Panthers' zone. She couldn't break free or turn. So she fired a backward pass between her legs right onto Mel's stick in the slot. Mel made no mistake and lifted a wrist shot over the goalie's shoulder.

As the Panthers player eased off, Zoey glanced to the stands. Her mother was cheering and clapping. Her father sat silent, though he was smiling.

It was a one-goal game.

Passes failing, number 18 tried to do it on her own. But Tia beat her to every loose puck.

With five minutes left in the second period, Zoey and Mel crossed the blue line on a two-on-one. Zoey faked a pass to fool number 4 into falling to the ice to block it. Then Zoey waited until she was past number 4's sliding body. She dished the puck to Mel, who whacked it into the mesh.

Mel skated to Zoey. "That one's for your dad," she said.

The game was tied.

Coach Mikom fired up the Sharks during the flood. "This is your year, girls!" he said. "You've worked hard and the win is within reach. But whatever happens out there, be proud of what you've done this year, because you were awesome."

The Final

The Panthers came on strong in the third period. They outplayed the Sharks and peppered Anika with pucks. But the Sharks goalie made saves with her pads, blocker, chest. She even knocked a sure goal away from the net with the shaft of her stick as she lay sprawled on her stomach.

With four minutes left in the game, Jan skated into the Panthers' end and dropped the puck to Marika. Sensing a chance, Zoey charged the net. Marika passed to Kat, who saw Zoey to the side of the net and blasted a slap-pass in her direction. Zoey deflected Kat's slap-pass into the net.

The Sharks were ahead by a goal. But they couldn't celebrate yet. There was work to do.

The Panthers came on strong. But they were stifled by Anika. Kat and Marika were rocks on defence, protecting the slot and the goal.

The Panthers pulled their goalie with two minutes left. But the Sharks stopped every attempt and Tia kept the puck from number 18.

With ten seconds left, Anika's elbow got a piece of number 4's hard shot from the point. It saved the game.

The buzzer rang. The Sharks were the Lower Lakes champions!

This time Kat was the first to jump on Zoey. Mel and the rest of the team piled on top. Everyone was smiling and cheering. Zoey had never felt as happy.

On her way off the ice, Zoey saw her mom high-fiving and hugging the parents of her teammates. But Zoey's dad was standing by himself.

In the lobby, Zoey went to her father. "Dad, it's okay to celebrate," she said. "We won!"

"I know, I know," said her dad. "I just didn't want to offend anybody or cause more trouble."

"Don't worry. All that's in the past. It's perfectly fine to cheer."

"Okay then," said her dad. "Way to gooo, Sharks!" Loosening up, he wrapped his daughter in a bear hug. "I'm so proud of you."

"I'm proud of you, too, Daddio. Thanks for everything."

Mel and Tia walked by and Zoey stopped them to meet her parents. "Guys, this is my mom and dad. They run the sweetest farm in all of Innisfil."

Mel and Tia smiled and said hello.

A beaming Coach Mikom told the Findleys that their daughter had played a tremendous game. "You've got a real hockey player there. And a great girl."

Zoey's mom thanked the coach for his kind words. Her dad told him now that his back was better, he'd be able to attend more games next season.

Coach Mikom lagged back with Zoey and Mel as Zoey's parents walked ahead. "Mel, there was a national team scout at the game today," he said. "He asked me about you. He thinks you've got great hands and natural scoring ability."

"That's great," said Mel. "But what about Zoey? She set up most of my goals this season."

"I know," said Coach Mikom. "I told him he'd better keep his eye on the two of you. And Kat and Anika, too."

"What did he say?" asked Mel.

"That he'd come to a few games next season and watch you all play."

"That's awesome," said Zoey.

Zoey couldn't wait for the new season to start. At home, excited and grateful, she wrote thank you letters to her sponsors. She wrote to the KidSport, youth-reach and JumpStart programs. She wrote a letter to Mr. Davis, the Canadian Tire store manager, and to Mr. Lopez of Lopez's Windows and Doors. Before she sealed the last letter, she dug out a copy of her hockey photo for Mr. Lopez to hang on his wall.

ACKNOWLEDGEMENTS

I would like to thank my editor at Lorimer, Kat Motosune, whose perceptive feedback and guidance improved my book immeasurably. She has a brilliant eye and is a pleasure to work with. Also, thanks to Sara D'Agostino for guiding the book through its final stages.

This story wouldn't exist without the inspiration of my two kids, Grace and Michael. Both were and are exceptional athletes and I was lucky to have had a front seat for their remarkable accomplishments and to have coached them occasionally.

I would also like to thank my father Michael O'Brien, for having been a great dad and encouraging my writing in my youth; and my wife Kit O'Brien, for having supported my writing quite literally since the year 2000.

And finally, I'd like to thank James Joyce, Virginia Woolf, Bruce Springsteen, Hayley Wickenheiser, Christine Sinclair, Sidney Crosby and Justin Williams — just for being awesome!

MORE SPORTS, MORE ACTION
WWW.LORIMER.CA

CHECK OUT THESE OTHER HOCKEY STORIES FROM LORIMER'S SPORTS STORIES SERIES:

Bench Brawl
By Trevor Kew

The "Helmets" and the "Gloves" have been rink rivals forever. When the league decides to merge the two teams to represent their small town at a big invitational hockey tournament in Vancouver, Luke and his friends are furious. Nothing is going right for the newly formed Great River Vikings — they seem to be more willing to fight among themselves than to battle against their opponents. Can the team come together to win it all for their hometown?

Called Up
By Steven Sandor

For David Timko, making the Bantam A hockey team is everything. So when he doesn't make the cut and is forced to play house league, his bad attitude soon gets him benched. His new friend Omar has problems of his own. A Syrian refugee, Omar's angry that his parents can't find good jobs in his new country or provide for him the way they used to. And he's desperately missing his older brother, who was left behind in Syria. As both boys become more frustrated with their own problems, their friendship begins to suffer. Can they come to understand each other's problems before their friendship comes to blows?

Cross-Check!
By Lorna Schultz Nicholson

Josh, Peter, and Sam are thrilled to be reunited at a hockey tournament in Kelowna, but a lot has changed. Sam now lives in Ottawa, Josh is dealing with his diabetes, Peter is becoming a major star, and all three boys play on different teams. Can they remain friends as they all compete to be in the gold medal game?

Delaying the Game
By Lorna Schultz Nicholson

All-girls hockey is a whole different world for Kaleigh — there are new teammates, new rules, and new problems to deal with. And when Shane comes along, Kaleigh finds that the world of boys has become just as confusing. Can she stick to her goals and rediscover her love for hockey, or will these distractions throw her off her game for good?

Empty Net
By David Starr

Madeline Snow is the star goalie and captain of her girls rep hockey team in Burnaby. So when her father moves the family to his new posting in a remote northern town she feels like she is losing a lot. Things begin to turn around when Maddie discovers she has made the town's only Bantam team, a boys team called the Stars, but since they have a skilled goalie in Connor Spencer, Maddie wonders if she will ever get to play. Can Maddie find her place in this new town and prove herself in net?

Ice Time
By David Trifunov

Paul Bidwell dreams of playing on a hockey team but knows that his mother can't afford to pay for the registration fees or the equipment. So he plays boot hockey with his friends and practices alone every night on the open-ice rink in the park. When the flu and mononucleosis hit Paul's school and his best friend, Vincent, is laid up with a concussion, an opening is created on Vincent's team, the Wildcats. Paul finally gets the chance to prove to the other players — and to himself — that he deserves his time on the ice.

Making Select
By Steven Barwin

Hockey is all Tyler ever wanted to do. But when he finally makes the Select team, things aren't how he imagined it. Tyler divides his time between playing for fun in house league and playing high-stakes hockey in Select. But trying to succeed at both is wearing him down. And the pressure isn't just coming from the players and the coach, it's coming from somewhere much closer to home — his hockey-loving mom. Tyler's burnt out and feeling crushed by the stress, but how can he give up the game he loves?

Stick Pick
By Steven Sandor

Star player Janine leads her hockey team to victory at the provincial championships. But on the way home from the game, a car accident leaves her paralyzed from the waist down. Her best friend and teammate, Rowena, urges Janine to look into sledge hockey. Adapting to her new life, Janine meets frustration at every turn. Soon Janine begins to appreciate her new sport. Her experiences lead her to speak up about rights for the disabled, taking her cause all the way to the professional sports arena. She might be a sledge hockey rookie, but she knows she's up for any challenge.